The Winter Name of God

The Winter Name of God

by

JAMES CARROLL

SHEED and WARD, Inc.
Subsidiary of Universal Press Syndicate
NEW YORK

ACKNOWLEDGMENTS

Grateful acknowledgment is made to the following sources for permission to quote from published material:

James Murray for permission to reprint "Death Poem" by Michele Murray from *The Great Mother and Other Poems*, copyright © 1974 by Sheed and Ward.

John Logan for permission to quote from his poem "Spring of the Thief," which appeared in the book *Spring of the Thief* published by Alfred A. Knopf, copyright © 1963 by John Logan.

Delacorte Press / Seymour Lawrence for excerpts from *Breakfast of Champions* by Kurt Vonnegut, Jr., copyright © 1973 by Kurt Vonnegut, Jr.

Thanks to Joe Cunneen for thoughtful suggestions and encouragement during the preparation of this book.

Library of Congress Catalog Card Number 74-34556

ISBN: 0-8362-0615-0

FOR
JOHN GEORGE LYNCH

The name of God is changing in our time.
What is his winter name?
Where was his winter home?

— John Logan
"Spring of the Thief"

CONTENTS

PART 1:   *Adventures of the Word*

    1: THRESHOLD STONE   3
    2: REMEMBRANCE   23
    3: TROUBLES   43

PART 2:   *Recovery*

    4: ABBA: DEAR FOLKS   63
    5: WORLD TOO MUCH WITH US   77
    6: THE NAME OF GOD   97
    7: FAMILY OF GOD   113

PART 3:   *Consequences*

    8: CONSECRATION   135
    9: WITH JESUS   149
    10: PRAYER   165

PART 4:   *Adieu*

    11: THE LAW OF RETURN   181

PART ONE
Adventures of the Word

⫽ 1 ⫽

Threshold Stone

It had something to do with God. Perhaps everything. Months, years of stifled outrage, confusion, and silence, a gradual loss of ease and comfort that made us "religious" once; it all left us changed, strangers to what we were.

By the early 1970s we had been through that remarkable sequence of exhilaration and despair that cost some men and women their lives, others their friends, some their country. All of us were out of breath. We were seeing differently. It was like being thrown up on the shore of a strange island. It was not home.

I am remembering my own moment of recovery. I am reliving it. The pieces were not fitting together in the old pattern. And one crucial one seemed to be missing; it had something to do with God.

I believe in God, the Father Almighty, Creator of Heaven and earth.... I grew up on those words. They nurtured me. They made me who I am. *And in Jesus Christ his only son, our Lord, who was conceived of the Holy Spir-*

it. . . . Was I going to be another of that long line of
people, good people surely, for whom belief, *that* belief,
had become another relic of another age, a memory of
childhood?

That was the question my life was putting to me. Was
belief to go the way of patriotism? Was my sense of myself
as a member of the church, as a Catholic, a son of God,
going to fade like the small pillar of smoke clowns balance
in their hands? Was this growing up?

*He suffered, died, and was buried. He descended into
hell.* . . . It was an age in which we all seemed to do
that. Descending into hell, a contemporary pastime. The
hell focused, of course, for us in the discovery that our
ease and comfort and "dream" were built on the misery
of millions. It was the discovery we made as the dreary
curse of Vietnam's nightly appearance on television
confronted us with the nightmare our dream had become.

I don't intend a treatise on the war. Nor another polemic
(though perhaps we need more of both). My concern is
simpler and more complex. My concern reaches only to
the effect this age, in all its violence and disillusion, has
had on the human capacity to believe. On, I should say,
my capacity to believe.

To believe what? In what? Not Buicks. Not salesmen.
Not new political visions. Not a cult of private purity.
To believe in God. To believe in God in the way of our
mothers and fathers in the faith. *This* faith. Christian
faith. The faith of the church. Can we keep it? *I believe
in the holy, catholic church, the communion of saints,
the forgiveness.* . . .

One crucial piece to my puzzle was missing. It had something to do with God. I noticed the lack as one winter turned spring into summer. Like a lot of other people, I saw the changing of the sixties to the seventies as if from within a storm. My life was a flurry of work and organization and pursuit. Now I'm not sure what it was we were doing, but we were doing it all the time. Consequently some questions, especially those born of silence and stillness and solitude, were not asked. We were, we said in our self-justification, ending a war. It was as if soul and heart and mind had to wait on the dying body of the earth.

But then something stopped. American soldiers came home. The focus of our effort evaporated as economic systems and habits of power went about the business of owning the world, but too subtly for our crude resistance. The lessons and commitments of our struggle for peace required faithfulness more than ever. But we learned suddenly that such faithfulness requires roots that reach to the soul. Roots in, one might say, a soil of belief that sustains, nurtures, holds the water in dry times. Something to do with God.

That winter of 1973 was a time when we dared finally to look at what we had become. I should speak for myself. When *I* finally looked I did not know myself. I did not know how I was American anymore. How I was free when teachers of mine, notably the Berrigans, were imprisoned. How I was religious when I couldn't seem to pray. How I was a priest when the church seemed alien in its concerns. How, finally, I was a believer in God when the words of the old creed rang hollow even as I said them.

The resurrection of the Body and life everlasting. Amen.
In another time, no doubt, spiritual sages would have recommended a "retreat." The disciplines of contemplation, holy books, the hours of prayer. Curiously enough, that strange winter made such a recommendation to me.

It came through the invitation of a monk in the Holy Land, offered through Paulist President Tom Stransky, to spend that coming summer at the monastery in a program of study and prayer. Israel. The sacred earth. War zones. Embattled Arabs and Jews. Remnants of the Temple. The daily life of Jesus. Desert lands. Golgotha. The empty tomb. Yes. I would go.

And I went. Fearfully. Gratefully. Self-consciously. I remember not wanting to be a tourist, but rather an adventurer and, perhaps, in a way, a pilgrim. Even as I sat alone in the passenger bar at JFK I was aware of the difference between me and the cheerful travelers. I nursed my drink and an idea of myself. I sat smoking, watching the others go off to holidays. Me? I was ascending the holy mountain. I was going to walk the sacred earth and find out for sure. I had an appointment with God; if He wasn't there I would know.

I thought of what I was leaving behind, had left behind already. I had been a college chaplain for nearly five years. Five years of claiming to nurture belief in young men and women, of inviting them to make the old creed theirs. Five years of hearing and speaking the Word in the midst of Babel. I had learned that there is no joy quite like that you experience when the Word of Truth comes from your mouth. And no pain either. There had been exquisite moments of belief and teaching in my short priesthood. The eyes of a student who understands the love of God

at last, understands at your urging, those eyes lit fires
in me. I loved it. Loved listening to them and eating with
them and watching them grow from my place of growing.
I loved being their friend and more; being a sign of
another friend, God. I loved being their priest.

But I had been thrown up on an alien beach. Sitting
in the airport bar on my way to Israel I understood, for
the first remembered time, that faith in God *could* be
lost. Or changed beyond meaning. Or outgrown. In any
case it could be left behind. I wondered if that was happening to me. At that moment even the words "lose
one's faith" suggested a world and a place in it that I
did not know.

I had cherished the Eucharist, for example. Cherished
my role in it as priest, breaker of bread, preacher of the
Word. But more and more a vast silence had crept into
my prayer. I had found myself pretending to address God
on the people's behalf. Pretending even to feel and believe
what was leaving me increasingly untouched. How do you
invite others to share pretense? How do you preach when
faith has become the unlimited silence? And how do you
share the precious gift of laughter when you take yourself
so seriously?

It was more than political issues, more than my embarrassment at the foibles and well-known corruptions of
the church. It was more than the self-consciousness all
priests should feel about their "good standing" in a male,
mostly white elite. It was more than my piece of the age's
assault on value and belief of whatever kind. It had, as
I started by saying, something to do with God. With
God's absence. None of the rest of my life would hold if
I could not sustain a sense of his nearness. More than

that, God's nearness had to be of the highest value if I
was to continue to be the man I thought I was.

God was not with me in that bar at JFK. Not in any
way I sensed. I was not, thankfully, beyond enjoying the
irony of that moment—young Father Carroll off for the
summer to the Holy Land. Clerical equivalent of the jet-
setter off to St. Moritz. The anguished young priest: "Ah,
yes, turning thirty does jade one's fervor, doesn't it?"
Poor fellow. And finally laughable. I had to admit it but
that didn't mean I could pretend that all was well. Like
the aristocrat who slips on a banana peel, the man of
prayer who does not know how to pray may in fact be
filling the role of a clown. But I still wanted to believe
in God.

They announced my flight. I drank up. I crushed the
cigarette. I fell into line with the tourists. But like Woody
Allen pretending to be Humphrey Bogart, I fancied that
I was different. Not a mere tourist but a pilgrim. An
adventurer of the Word. I had blown-up images of myself
that set me apart, cut me off. *That* was the essence of
what I was feeling. Maybe it was the airport or boarding
a plane; I always feel alone, set apart, utterly independent
at those places and times. Usually I don't mind.

But this time I did. As the big plane turned onto the
main runway and the pilot said, "Attendants be seated,"
I pushed my head back against the cushion and tried not
to imagine the plane crashing. But I couldn't help it.
Whenever I'm on a plane that's taking off I am overrun
by visions of the crash, the fire, the houses destroyed,
rescuers going through the ashes, policemen weeping, my
parents stunned at the word that I had died before they

did. So young. And in his prime. He showed such promise.

Rushing down the runway in the middle of a long silver tube with 180 others, I am always terrified. My palms wet, my eyes closed, I pretend to be asleep. I do not believe that airplanes can fly, though usually I pretend I do. Usually—that is, until I'm in one taking off. Since I don't believe in airplanes, those are moments when I believe in God. But this time, off to Israel, whatever the trick was that I'd played on my mind before, it didn't work. As that plane rushed toward the end of the earth, I could not muster trust. I could not commend my spirit. I could not say, "Whatever happens is OK with me." I did not want to die. I did not want to be hurled off the planet into nothing, into gas, into history. I wanted God to be there holding me, brushing my hair back from my face, humming. "But that's not God," I remember thinking, "that's Mom."

My mom is named Mary. (Her mother's name was Ann. My dad's name is Joseph. My initials are J.C. I take myself *very* seriously.) She believes in God. Every night when she goes to bed she says the rosary, a decade for each of her sons—Joe, Jim, Brian, Dennis, Kevin. She goes to Mass on weekends, kneels for communion though a vein swells in her knee, and is generally fond of priests. She is Irish, and her life takes its meaning from the religion of her people.

When my mother held me those years ago, part of what she held me with was God. I have memories of rocking in the old chair against her breast—the rocking, the breathing, the humming, the mother-smell, the beating of blood, the floating peace—memories that taught me heaven. Because Mom demonstrated her own peace by praying and talking to Mary the Mother of God as if they were sisters or the same woman—"Holy Mary," she'd say—I associated my act of belief with my act of love for that woman. And not only love, of course, but fear. I learned how to fear God by fearing her; *"Jesus, Mary, and Joseph,"* she'd holler when my brother or I was bad or she was tired. Cross her, I learned, and you cross God's mother. It was the secret of her power. But have her embrace and the very heart of the universe was yours. I learned faith in the cradle of her arms. It was as strong and sure as she was. God was as affectionate and as impatient. Jesus was one of the boys, and he was as subject to the conspiracy of mothers, of Marys, as I was.

But that was gone. I had grown up. Mom and I had done our duty to each other—separation, distance, agony. No Oedipal subjection, ultimately. No final dominance. It was like leaving Nazareth. The habit of affection clung even as I learned, partly at her bidding, partly in defiance, to be a man and a son both. But at that moment of leaving earth in a huge machine that had no right to fly, I knew that a mother's love, even the deep and unyielding love of my mom, is *not* the same thing as belief in God. My mother, finally, was not Saint Mary. Just Mary. Jesus was not one of the household. I was not flesh of God's flesh. I was a confused American male whose meanings had shifted radically with the times and who, at that moment, had more faith in Trans World Airlines than he had in the religious habits of his parents and of his own past.

The plane made it, of course. When the "No Smoking" sign went off and the chime sounded and the stewardesses began their bustling around the cabin, I stopped pushing back against the seat. My palms dried. I looked forward to a drink, put on my earphones, and waited for the movie.

It is nearly always possible to discuss the question of God's existence in a detached and friendly manner. Only when the fact of death as possibility, indeed as inevitability, is faced squarely does that issue become heart-rending, breath-stopping. The airplane's takeoff had been a moment like that for me. I did not know if I believed in God. I did not know if God was near. I did not want, of course, to die. But I did not want, above all, to die with a heart full of chaos, not knowing where I had come from or where I was going. I longed for the belief I had once held so easily. I was off to Israel to find it.

But I knew even then, at the beginning, that a search for *that* belief would be fruitless. The God of my youth was gone forever. That God I had also learned about in childhood from my father, whose life and faith had taught me as much as my mother's had. My dad is a tall, strong man whose Irish faith refuses the trappings of piety. But he has never to my knowledge missed Mass on a Sunday. And his sense of conscience, of duty, of responsibility before the throne of God, is tangible. Because he pursued two successful careers in government, with the FBI and with the Air Force, and because he has been in personal spirit and professional status a man of immense authority, I found it easy to identify his God with the received stereotype of a lawgiving, order-barking God who wanted submission from his creatures.

The God I had gotten from my father was no longer my God by the time I left on that plane. The years that had brought me to that moment had prepared me to prize rebellion above submission. The nature of the alliance between the God of religion and the powers of war had become all too clear. The priests I had grown up admiring had been military chaplains who represented, among other things, God's commitment to the American way. One of the privileged moments of our family life had come when we welcomed Cardinal Spellman into our Air Force home in Germany. The occasion was one of his Christmas visits to the troops, for whom he was chief chaplain, chief blesser, chief sign of God's fondness for our weapons.

Needless to say, my experience was not unique. The Vietnam war taught most Americans something new about themselves. But for me the transformation of political identification that occurred through even a marginal participation in "resistance," as we used to say, struck at the root of family relationships. It struck at the heart of who I thought God was.

Yes, I had been naive. Yes, my early faith was childish. Yes, it was silly of me to identify Cardinal Spellman's misguided commitments with the will of God. And yes, even now, it is impossible for me to say what sort of God the Air Force church believed in then and believes in now. But I *truly thought* that God was available to me and I to him by means of a sort of dedication that borrowed its language from the Bible but took its contemporary form in a version of the "American Dream."

As a college student, for example, I entered the seminary with the idea of becoming an Air Force chaplain. An officer. Blue uniform. Captain's bars. Salutes and all. By the time I was ordained seven years later, I knew what a nightmare for millions of others that "Dream" of mine implied. Still, I celebrated my first mass at the chapel of Bolling Air Force Base, and I was joined at the altar by several chaplains, including the general-priest who was the chief. We stood between the blue eagle of the Air Force and the flag of the United States of America. Even then I wanted out. When the base chaplain, welcoming the people, said how much he looked forward to my joining him in the blue uniform and the service of "the Free World," I remember hiding my face in my hand and asking to be forgiven the cowardice that kept me seated and silent.

We have our faith by hearing. By listening. We do not have it alone. I grew up listening to my people and believing as they did. Perhaps *because* they did. But by the time of the winter that led me to a summer in Israel, "my people" included others besides Mom, Dad, the base chaplain, Cardinal Spellman, and J. Edgar Hoover, who we knew *should* have been a Catholic. "My people" had come to include some whose "faith," if you could call it that, might have looked like atheism to my parents. Students, hippies, draft board raiders, men who had left the priesthood, women who swore they would never approach official Eucharist so long as their sisters were excluded from orders. "My people" also included Daniel Berrigan, who was the opposite of the chaplain-priest I had wanted once to become. And through him and others, I came increasingly to recognize outcasts and victims as "my people." The Vietnamese, struggling and faithful.

One day two FBI agents paid me a call. They were both Catholic, Knights of Columbus. Both polite. Both looking for a young man I knew. They reminded me of the other man I might have become (and in fact, one of my younger brothers had by then joined the FBI). I had myself worked summers during college as a clerk in the cryptanalysis section of the bureau. I had loved it. I had been one of them. I wondered if they knew.

"Well, Father," they said, "do you know where he is?"

"I guess not," I said. "I don't remember."

"Well, if you do remember, or if you hear anything, would you give us a call, Father? Here's our card." He held it out to me. I looked at it. I thought of my brother. Of my dad.

"Thanks," I said, not taking the card. "But I probably won't need it."

"Strange times, Father," the agent said, philosophic, tolerant. "I guess I don't understand what sort of creatures these draft dodgers and file burners are." He looked me hard in the eye, not expecting me to answer. But I said, though my only crime had been good citizenship, "We're human beings."

They left. I sat down at my big desk, feeling small, young, and newborn.

If my belief in God, my way of being religious, had changed, it had not changed because I had sat cross-legged listening to the wind. I had not watched something new from a fire tower. I had learned about conscience from agnostic students, and young women who a decade earlier might have become contemplative sisters had made me see the relationship between our bombing of Asian villages and the activities—and passivities—of the local church. At the university during those years we had had periodic visits from outraged police whose own frustration had fooled them into thinking their children were the enemy. When policemen and protestors spit at each other, though they share a nation and even a church, there is more than social science at stake. An idea of God is also at the center of the conflict. But no one—not the Boston Irish cop, nor the students, nor my fellow priests Michael Hunt and Jack Smith, nor my colleague Anne Walsh, nor Daniel Berrigan, nor my mom and dad, nor I—was able to say exactly what of God was at stake. By the time those days of the first phase of war against war had come to an end, all I knew was that I was changed. I found myself between ages. Between belief and disbelief.

When the community that mediates not only your idea of God but your sense of God's nearness falls apart, you start looking with new intensity for the church itself. There is no belief apart from church, and that may be the problem. The young men and women who spit out the established religious institutions, with their power-serving piety and fossils of "prayer," to have their mouths ready for the truth of a just and peaceable world—they are looking for the church. The cops and generals and Knights of Columbus agents and mothers of draft dodgers whose hearts ache at their children's "atheism"—they, too, are looking for the community that hands belief on to generations. They are looking for church too. "My people" includes them all somehow. My dad, whose God may or may not be mine, but whose strong, silent, kneeling blood beats through my body. My mom, who prays words I do not know, but in whose embrace I learned how to feed and breathe and listen to the ancient heart beating. I hear her now saying, "Jimmy, my Jimmy," and my soul still echoes with a voice of transcendent love. My mom and dad who teach me still, hold me still, send me out still to a new and angry world—they are my touch with the vast gathering of sisters and brothers we know as the past. They enable me to love it.

Even in ruins the past has its rights. And I knew on my way to the Holy Land monastery that the past had a right to me. To claim me. To demand that I be its eyes and ears and freedom in the present for the future. The past looks for church in us. And so, flying east, I moved from anger and collapse toward a world and a meaning that did not yet exist. I did so as one sent by my people.

I remember the feeling of exhilaration that came over me in the airplane. I was alone and confused and desperate for a word that would explain me to myself. But my growing awareness of the fact that the God of the past was not my God was the condition for creation, not despair. It was time to move beyond adolescent stereotypes and a piety that is deadly in its politics. Because the God of my parents had once been so marvelously mine I could move out of that world and that vision with at least as much strength as sadness. Because my folks had taught me how good it feels to have your small hand held by a big one, I could sit then, and for now, with my hands open and empty.

In Paris at Orly Airport they told me to put my hands up. We were changing planes. This was the security check for passengers bound for Tel Aviv. They had me in a small booth. The Israeli agent searched me thoroughly. I mustered all my docility. It was war, after all. They had to be careful, I supposed. Bombs and hijackings and all of that.

But then the agent found the small travel alarm clock in my bag. He handed it to me.

"Make it ring!" he said. I took it, wanting to say, "Come on, it's only me." But he was deadly serious. I fumbled at the tiny knobs on the back of the clock. I had always had trouble setting it.

"What kind of a bomb could this be?" I wondered, but said nothing. The guard was watching me. I was getting nervous now, beginning to perspire. "Tricky little thing," I said casually. He continued watching but took a step back from me. My God, I thought, he really thinks it's a damn bomb. But I still couldn't get it to work. Turning first the hands of the clock. Then the alarm needle. Then the hands. What the hell. Maybe somebody *had* switched clocks on me. Some desperado on the plane from New York or in the men's room. Maybe it *was* a bomb. I looked at the agent. He was looking at me. And when I looked again at the little clock, it exploded. I mean it rang. I jumped a foot off the ground. Then smiled at the man. "See?" I muttered.

"Thank you," he said. "Move on, please."

"Yes. Right." And I walked away thinking, God, this *is* war. These fellows don't mess around. It was my first lesson in the meaning of Israel.

I had a lot to learn. All my remembered days there had been *two* places called Israel. One was ancient Palestine, the Nazareth-Samaria-Galilee where the first Jews and Jesus lived. *That* Israel, as I thought of it, was all shrines and temples and synagogues. And somehow *that* Israel was where, even now, God had his headquarters. It was the "Holy Land," the piece of earth on which human beings had first uttered the cry of belief, the piece of earth on which God had walked. The *other* Israel was all soldiers and desert foxes, Arabs and Jews—each stereotyped—at one another's throats.

Arriving in Israel, I knew immediately that I was not

prepared to be there. I was shocked by the soldiers with their automatic weapons, looking at you, staring. The muzzle of a huge tank gun greeted us as we got off the 707. Inside the terminal a plaque marked the area where dozens of civilians had been shot by terrorists the year before. Good God, I thought, they could do it to me.

I quickly retrieved my bag, changed some money, and found a phone. I would call the monks. I would tell them I was here. I would find out how to get there. But I couldn't make the phone work. Between my clumsiness with the strange money and the shock of discovering that no, indeed, not all phone operators speak English, I was helpless. People were waiting to use the phone. No one had ever heard of the village I had scribbled in my book. People seemed to be watching me. All at once I had the strong sensation that the soldiers and the passengers and the terminal personnel and the woman waiting for the phone—that they all knew I was chaos inside where order is supposed to be. They all knew I was between belief and disbelief. I was not one of them. I was, maybe, gone from faith. I left the terminal, rushing into the hot after-noon. I stood on a patch of dirt, dropped my bag, stamped my feet, and said, not out loud, "O.K., Land, do your number on me. Make *me* holy. Help me find it. Help me believe."

I took a Jewish bus to Jerusalem, an Arab cab to the Arab quarter, an Arab bus to the monastery village, and I walked the mile of desert road to the monks' house. I arrived at twilight. The sky was beautiful. The door was open. The monks were eating in the refectory. I looked in on them, but they remained silent. Finally, one of them got up and showed me to a room. I thanked him. He left.

The room had a cross on the wall, a desk, a chair, and a bed, onto which I fell, wanting to weep. I managed not to—merely shuddered once and fell asleep.

Next day I began my tours of holy places. Tours by bus. Me and a bevy of tourists. Instamatic maniacs who swooned at shepherds and gave pennies to children, the cute ones. They fed crackers to cats and giggled when the guards winked. We went everywhere in single file, past tombs and ancient olive presses, and collected stone weapons. We went in and out of churches, and the guide was always kneeling down and saying "Hail Mary" and waiting for us to do likewise. I was embarrassed. I stayed on the bus half the time, pretending to be asleep. Pretending to be a wheel.

At Bethlehem, where Jesus Christ was born, I nearly died. I refused to stand with the others and sing carols as if it were Christmas. I refused to kiss the Greek altar with its coated incense. When they asked the priests present to come forward to celebrate the mandatory mass, I could not move, but stood there stark in my own ice, though it was summer. I was nearly frozen by my inability, in that crumbling basilica, to summon anything but cynicism up from my heart. There was a plaque on the stone floor that said, "Hic Incarnatus Est." I read it quickly and walked back to the monastery alone.

The next day was different. I had a cynic for a guide, an old Frenchman who was an archaeologist and a biblical scholar. He led me and a few others up and down the haunted streets of Jerusalem. Jerusalem. Though he was old, he flew ahead of us from shrine to shrine. No sentimentalist, he made no claims of certainty. He dismissed the pious legends of tourists and was consistently careful to qualify his reports with "Perhaps . . . near here . . . Jesus *may* have . . . who knows?" As I followed him through the relics and ruins, past Bethany, up the Mount of Ascension, into the Valley of Death, up the Mount of Olives, into Gethsemane, down the narrow alleys of the Arab market to the Sepulcher, I saw him snicker at the pious, spit toward the priests who were selling trinkets, ignore the soldiers, and gesture rudely toward commercial guides. I wondered what *he* believed. Was it all a museum to him? What difference did it make?

At the Holy Sepulcher I tried to imagine the death of Jesus. But all I could see were the warring monks, the bad art, the dollar candles, the tourists. The old Frenchman hovered in a corner while I tried to feel something about the place where, they say, God's son died. At the other end of the church, inside what looked like a large, elaborate kiosk, there was the entrance to the tomb. I went into it and found that it was not empty. A sad-eyed salesman-monk was waiting in the tomb to see if I would buy a candle from him, or perhaps a plastic cross. The poor man, I thought. Such death on legs. Where was resurrection in this?

At the end of the day the old Frenchman took us to one final place. Oh, well, what did I have to lose? What *left* to lose? I had come, it seemed to me at that point, face to face with my own unbelief. With my distance from the places and words and rituals that were at the heart of the tradition.

We went into a private house, a big place only a few hundred years old in the center of the ancient city. We followed our guide down corridors and stairs, bumping our heads, getting dirty. We went down into an excavation that was being dug beneath the big house. It was well lit. We could see the large stones of an ancient wall. The Frenchman gathered us in a corner. "Here, here," he said, gesturing, impatient. We pushed close to him. He pointed to the ground; we cleared a space. There was a large stone slab about nine feet long and three feet wide. It was unremarkable. An ordinary stone. We looked at it in silence. No one spoke for a long time. We sensed the change in the Frenchman, who stood, hunched, staring. Finally he said, barely audibly, "This was the threshold stone of the city gate in the time of Herod. . . . Here you see the city wall. . . . It is certain that Jesus of Nazareth stepped on this stone with his feet when he left the city to die."

"Ah, Jesus Christ have mercy on me." I knelt. I bent forward. I kissed the stone that his foot had touched. I understood then that the mystery of existence itself had brought *me* to a threshold. A place to cross. A way to leave the city and enter it. I wanted more than anything else in memory to do my crossing with Jesus Christ. Whom I still did not see then, there. At that stone. In the eyes of the Frenchman. In the company of my fellow tourists. I did not see Jesus. But I saw them. And I imagined words that he would say to such sentiments as I had then: "Cross with me? Not this stone, James. Not this gate. This is the one, as I learned, you cross alone."

⫼ 2 ⫼

Remembrance

I remember them saying, as I had said myself, that all we know of God is revealed in Jesus Christ. I arrived in the Holy Land wanting to believe that but not knowing what it meant. My memory of Jesus by that time was vague, formless, half-dead. I used his name, half in prayer, half in vain. I knew the details of his story. I appealed to his prison history as justification for my politics. I rattled on in sermons about his call for commitment to the poor. He was the "liberator" *par excellence*. The great resister.

Though I myself had invoked it in such ways, I squirmed at the use so many others made of his memory. To me they were Jesus idolators, turning him into the long-haired freak, the fundamentalist bible-slapper, the flower child, the puppy lover, the magician. But when it came to the test, I could not pretend that I knew Jesus at all, or that my use of his memory differed from theirs at all. The content of my belief in Jesus bordered on floating sentiment, and I went crazily from rejection of his memory to rebellion in its name.

When I knelt at the threshold stone of the old wall, when I put my hand on the place where he had walked, I knew *this* was what I'd come to Israel for—to touch Jesus Christ, perhaps for the first time. What was required of me was an act of discipline, study, and silence that would do justice to my people's memory of the man of Nazareth. Whatever hope I had that a new Word of God, or a new prayer, would emerge from the chaos of shaken faith rested on the claims that my past made on me in the name of Jesus.

I found myself living in a monks' house that was halfway between Bethlehem and Jerusalem. Halfway, I understood at once, between birth and death. Halfway, I suspected, between belief and disbelief. There was an old gate, a meandering stone wall, an ancient grove of olive trees, a running fountain of water. In the chapel there were Greek icons of a Jesus whose eyes were all accusation. I did not kneel to them.

What little I saw of Jesus was from the hill. I traced the road with my eyes, not accusing, from the village where he was born to the city where he died. Between the village and the city the Judean desert lapped at comfort like a tide. I stood in the crossed shadow of the cave and the hill and knew that the man who had lived *here* had had chaos in *his* heart. I remember saying to the wind, "I want to listen to this place, to its memory. I want to find in the heart of my revolt an act of obedience."

I ran my eye up and down the far hills of the desert, brown, bald, alive with heat. In the distance were the ruins of Herod's castle. I tried to imagine John the Baptist, wandering at night, stealing fruit, almost crazy with loneliness. My mind even made pictures of Jesus, kneeling, running from the devil, hiding from the people. The desert land itself spoke of collapsed meanings, of terrors that the city denies, but that were strangely familiar. The Jesus who lived *here*, who lost himself, who doubted the elders, who went hungry, who lived on the edge of lost belief—I would listen to him. I longed to see my days in his. I looked at Bethlehem, turned, and looked again. Human beings had waited and watched here for centuries, for millennia; I would be one of them. I was watching and waiting for the Coming. The Coming of Truth and its Word. A name for what we had become. And for our longing.

I turned and went into the stone monastery. My monk's room, stark and white, with a bed, a table, a cross on the wall, had been prepared for me by four thousand years of patience. For a while the silence would be mine. I sat at the table and opened the Bible, hoping the book would open its secrets to me.

Of course, it didn't. The Bible is jealous of its secrets. Off and on, throughout my adult life, I had turned to the Scriptures, full of resolutions and all too quick with a commentary. I would make use of this new opportunity and become a man of the Word of God at last—a Christian who is not versed in the Scriptures is, after all, like an Irish poet who doesn't understand James Joyce. In this fever of good intentions I spent a few days doing nothing but Bible-reading before finally admitting that I was bored. What I needed was a drink. A mile down the road I found an Arab bar.

"Hello. You speak English?"

"Sure. Come in. You tourist? You wanna' guide?"

"No. Just a beer. You gotta beer?"

"Yes. Have a beer, mister. You American?"

"Yea."

"Hey, I gotta nephew in Minneapolis. You know Minneapolis?"

"Sure. I went to school there."

"Hey! University? My nephew's in university."

"No kidding? I went there."

"Here. Have the beer. Don't pay. You are welcome."

And I was. I went there often. I touched the ordinary experience of a man and his friends who made a life of welcoming strangers. They lived in a place where widely different cultures met, mixed, challenged each other. The barkeeper—Arab, Christian, primitive, modern, jovial, despairing, another of us whose certainties were continually shifting. His name was Abu. He lived on the tourist road, near ruins of temples and basilicas, where extraordinary religious faith mingled with the crassest sentimental exploitation. He lived in daily fear of warfare, subject to soldiers' stares, burdened by the memory of slaughtered children, Arab and Jew.

In his bar there was intense and nervous conversation, but the questions were not about the meaning of life, just the passing day. What difference did it make? Why was one asking, anyway? Out of season there were workers, shepherds, farmers, an occasional stranger who was welcomed. All sharing in the talk about the weather and the crops and the neighbors, a way in which ordinary people always hide their panic over forgotten meanings and their pleasure at the casual fellowship that survives every crisis.

It could not have been so different in Jesus' time. There were arrangements about where they would stay, what there was to eat, and long, quiet hours together. Was it merely idle to imagine Jesus employing the details of such "aimless" conversations to hide his fear of lost meanings and his pleasure in companionship?

Finally I returned to the Bible, determined not to lose myself in scholarship but to learn Jesus in his ordinary meanings. Nevertheless, some familiarity with scholarship was necessary if I was to get beyond the trite familiarity that had deadened my knowledge of the Gospels. And I would submit to the formal rituals of monastic hours, avoiding the eyes of the icon. But also, and mainly, I would test what I read with Abu and his fellows at the bar, and with the memory of those at home with whom I had shared the panics and pleasures of an age.

I chose to focus my reflections on the Gospel of John—as it turned out, on a particular passage of it. What I knew of the memory of Jesus enshrined in John had always been attractive to me—the compassion, the open affection, the eloquence of its poetry, and even the suggestions of humor (I've the habit of reading into the text a kind of comic conflict between "the one whom Jesus loved" and "Simon, son of John, who betrayed him"). Rereading it now, I began to discover that this Gospel records an experience of Jesus that has special significance for people whose belief is undergoing the radical bounce between alienation and creativity.

The chaos and readiness to think new thoughts that we associate, often parochially, with our times, were reflected just as clearly in the religious consciousness of the people whose experience the Gospel of John records. To locate that experience in the historical moment, it is helpful to recall the cultural ecology of the Gospel, even at the risk of some generalization.

One of the important events for us of the time we're concerned with was the radical declericalization among Jews that accompanied the destruction of the Temple in A.D. 70. It had been the center of cult and priesthood, and the shape of Jewish religious observance was drastically altered by the loss of it. Suddenly and for good the religious *place* was gone and the meaning of the religious *person* as cultic worshipper was changed.

The brutal and idolatrous Roman power that brought about this change engendered among the Jews a new political-religious radicalism that made revolt an act of piety. The last overt movement of religious-political revolt was crushed at Jerusalem and at the Jews' last stand at Masada in A.D. 73.

Masada is a high desert mountain overlooking the Dead Sea. I climbed it one morning beginning at dawn. The narrow ledges, the intense, burning sun, the vast emptiness, the thirst that still kills people—it had been the last refuge of a people's hope. I remember standing on the pinnacle of the fortress whose ruins still seem alive with the valiant resistance of those Jews. Below, there were still traces of Roman camps from which the siege had been mounted. It was easy to imagine the assaulting soldiers, the flung fire, the cries and curses, and suddenly I knew that my loss, my burden, was nothing compared to that. But, just as suddenly, I knew that real belief was nothing without its test. If people who thought of themselves as God's had been blasphemed, pillaged, raped, murdered, ripped from their meanings by a crazed army of empire, there was special reason, in our banal desperation, to listen to them, remember them, carry them with us. One has to be almost shameless to compare oneself to the resisters of Masada, but my roots are in what they did, in what they believed, in what they died for.

The first Christians had to discover the meaning of their belief amidst the destruction of the Temple and persecution by the Romans. They had to measure their commitment against the radical demands of Jesus, who, even if he was not one of them was not untouched by the political dreams of the zealots. If the resisters at Masada had to reclaim their religious identity in a wholly new way, so did his disciples.

The person who chose to follow Jesus submitted to a further test of mind and soul that makes ours—mine—seem trivial by comparison. The call to follow Jesus was a call to be a new kind of Jew; to accept him as the long-awaited but unexpected Messias entailed a profound shift in religious consciousness. The shift in religious consciousness required of a Jew who would follow Jesus as the expected Messias was probably as immense and traumatic as the movement today from orthodox belief to atheism. The ground had moved under one's feet; nothing was what it had seemed to be before.

I think, for example, of the "great number of Jewish priests" who, according to Acts 6:7, adopted the Way of Jesus. They lost both their priestly identity and religious role on entering a community in which ministries were neither clericalized nor elitist (not yet, at least). It must have been like leaving the Catholic priesthood, the Catholic Church, and one's immediate family, all at once.

It is a sign of how we domesticate the memory of our people, purging it of the conflict we experience, that I should have been surprised to think of early Christians feeling such a "contemporary" sense of division and agony in coming to a new basis of belief. Such arrogance to assume that we are the first to be at a loss about religious practice and meaning! It is important to remember that Christianity was *born* in turmoil and *built* on a break with the most traditional and sacred ideas about God. It is so easy to forget that the first followers of Jesus did not attach taboos to material things, religious buildings, times, or persons. Though we have spent a couple of thousand years ignoring it, Jesus was *condemned* for rejecting the material Temple in favor of the temple of living stones (John 2:19).

The irony of taking the tradition seriously at a moment of revolt like ours is that the same act of revolt is at the source of the tradition. It is not for nothing that in Rome the followers of the Way were regarded as atheists. Nor is it for nothing that increasing numbers of people, young and old, are today unable to use language about God that has been hallowed by centuries of religious custom. Could it be that Catholics who "leave the priesthood" or "religious life" or who stop "going to Mass" are expressing inarticulately the same resistance to idolatry that led Jesus out of the Temple precincts? Perhaps the first act of rebellion against fossilized clerical structures has to be an act of remembrance: we need to get closer to the reality of that rebellion, political and religious, from which Christianity itself issues. Of course, "leaving the priesthood" or "stopping attendance at Mass" or "losing one's faith" are not in themselves signs of liberation; these choices may in turn represent a superficial accomodation to fashion or a concession to the pursuit of comfort. To go beyond such caricatures, one has no choice but to embrace in a new way the roots of tradition. To meet Jesus again and, especially, to understand how his first followers, who, after all, are *our* people too, understood and interpreted his meaning for their times.

We soon learn, however, that the record of the first Christian memories of Jesus, the New Testament, is itself filled with ambiguities and conflicts. The scholar's contribution lies in the opening that occurs when complexities are sorted out and put in perspective. Compiled and developed over decades, the New Testament includes its own reinterpretations—as the scholar might say, its own *midrash*.

Midrash was the habit, developed by Israel over centuries, of retelling the old story of God's saving acts. Israel's Scriptures record its people's journeys from trauma to trauma, from crisis and collapse to victory and rebirth—their coming home and their being carried off to exile again. The immense range of experience that a uniquely chosen people had survived shaped the stunning language they called God's Word. When the language they inherited from their mothers and fathers proved inadequate to their new experience, they fell silent for a time, then set about reinterpreting the old language in the light of the new experience. This reinterpretation out of silence is the act of *midrash*.

The inherited language said God was mighty—but his enemies destroyed his Temple. And Jeremiah said, "God does not evoke awe in the forces that destroy his temple. I am silent." For Moses, whose experience had been escape from Egypt, God's might meant his absolute power over history. But for Jeremiah, whose experience was defeat and exile, God's might meant prolonged suffering, his mysterious decisions to be defeated by history. The question for the Jews had once been, "Who is as powerful as God?" After exile it became, "Who is as silent as God?"

In our time the Jewish face of God has shifted again. After six million people died, many of them passively, Israel began to prize in a new way the act of resistance. Of defiance. A long-suffering God, a defeated God, called forth a piety that led to boxcars and lethal showers. That God is gone for Israel. In the name of the new God, Israelis proclaim, "No more Masadas!" No more defeats! History has altered religious meaning.

The religious meanings of the first generations of Christians were altered by history in equally radical ways. The record of those decades reflects the continuing habit of *midrash,* the sense those people had that they were bound to retell and reinterpret the memories they inherited. Thus the experience of the second and third generation people who had not known Jesus when he walked the earth required a rebellion against the memory of those first generation people who had. Things kept changing, and as they did what was needed of the one regarded as Redeemer changed too.

What has happened to us in the collapse and shift in our faith also happened to them. It is the human experience. No one owns God. When we blandly affirm that God is involved with history, we are simultaneously asserting that knowledge of God, language about God, and worship before God can and do change drastically with the times. Such a way of viewing reality seems self-evident in the Scriptures, once we give up the idea of an imprisoning tradition, yet its implications constantly remain fresh. When I finally understood this habit of past believers, I was delighted: *here* was a way of understanding what was happening to *me*. That my experience was out of synch with my memory of faith did not, after all, make me wrong, or fallen away. It only made me stop for a while, before beginning the task of *midrash* for my times and places. Reinterpreting, telling the story again. Going from silence to a new Word.

I turned to John's Gospel as part of the record of rebellion against the earliest memories the people had of Jesus. The reinterpretation of Jesus' significance that John records was radically new, the product of a conflict, personal and ideological, equal to anything we know now.

Putting it too simply, at the risk of generalization, the first Christians thought of Jesus as the Messias who was establishing the earthly kingdom of peace and justice. Though he disappeared after the death-resurrection event, they fully and confidently expected him to come right back and finish what he had begun.

Well, of course, he didn't come back. Not that year. Not the year after. They'd gotten it wrong, or something. Some son must have challenged his father: "What are you talking about? It's sixty-four years you've been waiting!" And the father would have replied, "Well I don't know what to say. I'm silent."

Out of that silence, after the challenge to past ideas that only present experience can offer, a new notion of Jesus emerges. The reinterpretation that occurs in John suggests that the Messianic Age was not only begun by Jesus, but already completed. The people experienced the fact that Jesus was not returning that year or the year after. If his memory was to continue to have any meaning, it had to be reinterpreted.

The genius—one might say inspiration—of *midrash* is that it is true, even while effecting change, to the core insight of the earlier proclamation. John's thought is as return-oriented as the first memories of Jesus were, but in a radically different way. The predominant eschatological contrast elsewhere in the New Testament is a temporal one—the present age in contrast with the age to come, the same contrast we are familiar with in our own lives as *now* versus *then*.

In John the contrast is between two orders of existence, between what religious language calls the "temporal" and the "eternal." When the contrast is defined in these terms rather than within the merely temporal context, a wrenching loose from the frameworks of the past is required. John is inviting a new kind of perception, a new sense of what reality is and what experience points to. It is a shift in consciousness that approximates the shift in our own time from linear thinking, which is characterized as horizontal, sequential, and rational, to immediate thinking, which is vertical, simultaneous, and intuitive. The conflict was not resolved in the New Testament. In fact, the reinterpretation proposed by the people whose intuition John records was never fully accepted by Christians. Even now, conflicts in belief and politics can often be seen as contemporary versions of this same conflict, which is at the heart of the Gospel's meaning.

The differences implied in the rebellion of the children against the parents, as recorded in John, are evident in the conflict over such key concepts as *life, judgment,* and *glory.*

For John "eternal life" (3:36; 5:24; 6:47) has the sense of "life to the full." It is the instinct that God calls the people to nurture, protect, and celebrate the lives they live *now*, not in some future state. There is no discontinuity between what is given and what is promised. This means that the utterly ordinary events of human life— eating, making love, growing up, waking, wandering, wondering—are invested with ultimate significance. The simplest act of human life takes on the meaning of transcendence, for the act of life is itself the encounter with God. The central Christian notion of incarnation means that God has chosen to make himself available to people in their very breathing. In the simplest acts of their lives, even in having a drink with their friends.

And so I would slip out of the monastery at night and make my way to Abu's cafe. The smoky room, the laughter, the dirty stories, the bottled beer, the littered conversation, the lack of pretense—it was all its own justification. My attraction to the place was not concupiscence, nor merely respite from "holiness," but part of my increasing awareness that such ordinary, pleasant moments are every bit as graced as the other moments of "prayer." Abu's bar and the ancient stones of a monk's cell can equally claim to be God's household.

The contemporary piety that insists on locating ultimate significance exclusively in religion and holiness in church buildings has its equivalent in the New Testament, where "eternal life" most often has the sense of "life then." Life with God, life to the full, begins later, when the next world begins. Present activity—drinking, making friends, writing poems—is necessary but "profane." We meet God, according to this sensibility, by transcending what is ordinary.

You may have to slip off to the bar at night for fellowship or alcohol or both, but if you were "holier" or "closer to God," you wouldn't. The future-age orientation of this piety leads to the massive suspicion of life's daily pleasures that many associate with Christianity. The Gospel of John represents the opposite, the sense that life's daily pleasures, finally, are all we know of the God whose Word is flesh.

John's proposal for reinterpreting the meaning of Jesus' words about "eternal life" has immediate political consequences. As long as human significance is associated with future fulfillment, one can justify the callous disregard of present suffering, or even the exacerbation of it. The political critique of common piety as "pie in the sky by and by," for which Marx and others are noted, is already implicit in John's critique of earlier New Testament notions about "eternal life." In my own experience, the holiness urged upon us has almost always been an act of temporal expectation, and only rarely the cultivation of a deeper present existence for ourselves and others. My anger at a church whose righteous indifference to the present suffering of three-quarters of humanity has made it accessory to the crimes of power seems suddenly to be justified by the very roots of Christian belief.

For John, "judgment" is also a present event. The truth of our situation has its effects on us now, whether we know it or not. Elsewhere in the New Testament (Matt. 10:15; 11:22; Heb. 9:27) judgment is expected to occur in the future age. With such an orientation we spend our lives getting ready for *that* moment, for *that* encounter with God. But such a sensibility in effect devalues every moment, and the contemporary tendency to treat every experience as a means to some other, more profound experience (for example, the way education becomes a means toward career, which becomes a means toward social status, which becomes a means toward power, which becomes...) has here its theological undergirding.

When John writes, "Whoever does not believe has already been judged" (3:18), he is proposing that, as Camus put it, "the last judgment takes place everyday, my friend." In this perspective every moment of our existence takes on immeasurably more significance, for any moment can be the moment of ultimate meeting between our true selves and God. Every experience claims its right to be its own end, to be grasped as loaded with dread and with wonderful possibilities. It is easy to understand the appeal of a piety in which judgment is postponed, for the power and the freedom and the meaning that are implanted in the commonest choices can be a burden almost beyond our ability to carry. But the devaluing of present experience implied by this piety is exactly what leaves us bored and wondering in the end if anything matters at all. John's notion of judgment suggests that everything matters profoundly.

And so I set about to move through this day as if *it* were judgment day. I read the news and let it wrench me up from that absentee paralysis in which the choices of worldwide death and life are left to others. In my heart I carry the drought that kills brothers and sisters I have never met. I go for a walk, greeting a stranger as if she were God. I eat my lunch as the pleasure it is, and not as merely habit or duty. I work at my desk as if the task will make a difference to me and others. I play tennis, badly, angrily, smoke, and ask forgiveness. I make phone calls, visit friends, listen to the news, and think of my part in the web of lies that chokes the nation. I live a day as if the Russian proverb were mine: one word of truth outweighs the world. Yes, I say, but know from the weight I take how much I continue to fail. The last judgment, my friend, it happened today. There is nothing to do but go to bed, shudder once, and sleep well.

And "glory"; John's reinterpretation is revealed in this idea too. The glory of Jesus is usually regarded as what happens to Jesus after (temporally) his humiliation, torture, and death (Matt. 24:30; Phil. 2:5-11; Mark 13:26). It's the way we think of our own lives, dividing them into rewards and punishments, hills and valleys, ups and downs. The trouble is we spend most of our time on the way from one to the other, neither enjoying nor suffering so much as anticipating what comes next. Hell is anticipation, endlessly. For most of us, of course, it is an old habit.

John regards the very crucifixion of Christ as his glorification (7:39; 12:23; 17:1). His whole life was pointed to the one event of "being lifted up" (3:14; 8:28; 12:32), which is two acts of existence—crucifixion and resurrection—in one moment. The difference for John between the death and new life of Jesus is not temporal, but is a question of how deeply one plunges into existence. John's proclamation moves beyond the sequential promises of punishment and reward and says that the heart of Christ's death is life itself. There is glory in the curse; it only waits to be uncovered.

I remember the shock and disappointment I felt when I entered the Holy Sepulcher for the first time. *This* was glory? *This* was resurrection? All I saw were surly monks who tried to sell you candles, tour-guides who hustled tired pilgrims in and out of altar-rooms, weeping sentimentalists, and bored soldiers with their machine guns, eyeing Arabs. The walls were crumbling because the various religious factions that controlled the place could not cooperate in the repair. Moslems owned the land the basilica stood on; Jews governed it; Christians fought over it. While tourists gawked, I fled—no glory here! This is the empty tomb?

Later I visited another shrine in Jerusalem that is said to be the tomb of Christ. It was perfect. Called the "garden tomb," it has been pronounced the authentic site by English fundamentalist Christians who presumably, like me, had found the Holy Sepulcher scandalous, impious, and literally unbelievable. These English Christians found an ancient tomb in a lovely garden far removed from the chaos of the city. It was pretty and the attendants were polite and you could meditate there all day. There was even a big stone that might once have rolled back. You could just *see* those Roman soldiers trembling. It was all like a picture from an illustrated Bible, a memorial to "glory." In the end this resurrection museum drove me back to the crumbling church.

For the first remembered time I understood that the glorification of Jesus had occurred in a *human* setting, with all its chaos, treason, and crumbling ruins. Resurrection does not domesticate crucifixion or undo it or deny that it happens continually. The Holy Sepulcher is a sacrament of Christ's part in *our* destinies, for it is *we* who live in crumbling cities; *we* are the surly monks, the sentimental pilgrims, and the bored soldiers, and *we* are the ones who put the world to death and in whom it is reborn. The glory we seek is *here,* exactly. And the glory Jesus sought was exactly in the flesh he became as one of us. It is the scandal of glory, the glory of scandal. We go through life looking for God, carrying God on our backs.

The memory of Jesus as John interprets it (and as I understand it) reflected my experience of myself and my world. The commitment to the unity of polarities, the resistance against the dichotomizing that follows from a temporal, linear mind-set made me want to see Jesus again through the eyes of the Evangelist. I was looking for a way to understand the contradictions that I carried in my bones. When I arrived in Israel, they were clinging to me, nearly paralyzing me. I discovered in myself both life and death, as old loyalties faded and new meanings came. I was both victim and slayer, for I recognized myself as accomplice in the American violence that was even then being visited on my distant Asian family. I was a composite of glory and curses, bouncing in one day from the exquisite pleasure of a life well lived to the anguish that is its own shame when one suffers as little *real* tragedy as I. Similarly, I contained at once belief and disbelief—certain that the God of my previous ordered faith was gone, useless, even an enemy, while sensing also that I touch daily with my very flesh a spirit-being whose will is my peace.

I was looking for a way to live without being broken by such divisions. To live in a way that would allow both sides of myself their rights, so that, in my shuttle between Abu's bar and a monk's cell, I could claim to be continually in the presence of God. I turned toward John's Jesus as leaves in the morning turn toward the sun. The man described there was one of us. He would be with us drinking until dawn. He would cook us omelets on the beach and mock our piety. He would rebuke our ease with lies, never allowing us to forget the hunger stalking bodies and souls. He would show us not only how to pray but how to doubt. Only after making atheists of all of us would he teach us new names for the being who seemed so far away and yet a part of ourselves. And we would be quiet with him. And he would laugh at the lines we could never remember.

Troubles

So we are sitting at this bar. It is 1:30 in the morning. We have been telling each other the usual lies all evening. We have been trading pictures of ourselves in control, cool, winning games, making deals, on the brink of big success. One of us is a teacher with brilliant students, another a builder of roads and bridges, still another an athlete about to reach his peak. One of us is an organizer who cannot be bought off, another is a cop who is never afraid, another a lawyer who has his principles, another a farmer who loves the earth. And one of us is a priest who never lies in sermons.

Listen! Do you believe at last? The time will come—in fact it has come already—when you will be scattered, each going his own way and leaving me alone. And yet I am not alone because the Father is with me. I have told you all this so that you may find peace in me. In the world you will have trouble, but be brave. I have conquered the world. (John 16:32-33)

Cutting through pretense, the false images of the frightened male, his cool control, are these harsh words of Jesus. Cutting through my own glib sermon to myself on the Gospel of John. Don't pretend that aches are so easily rubbed away! Don't hypnotize yourself with piety! Jesus himself warns you: *you will have trouble!* Indeed, the first consequence of belief itself—*Do you believe at last?*—is trouble. Get ready for tough times. Don't assume that the world's broken heart will be healed when you get (1) a new job, (2) a new economic order, (3) a government with a conscience, (4) a new dose of holiness.

Your search for community, for example. There are forces and systems that make sustained common life over the long haul nearly impossible. You will be subject to them. Be sure of this: *you will be scattered!*

I remember the grand alliances that we made in the late sixties. We were the new breed, the new community, the new politics. We were going to end the war and change the church and get the world ready never again to be wrong and, all the while, love each other well. We were priests and anti-war activists and sisters and liberal families. We met in prayer groups, at demonstrations, at potluck suppers every other Tuesday. We went to the mayor's office to demand playgrounds instead of parking lots. We formed tenants' unions, threw block parties, and registered voters. We knew the names of communities like ours all over the country. We were rebirth itself. We were the *new* left, the conspiracy to save lives.

We were fools. We were naive about (1) the massive indifference of social structures to our will, and (2) the deadly, irrational resentment against other people that each of us carried in his heart. Yes, we were the Kent

State students murdered by the government. But we
were also the Weatherpeople who blew ourselves up in
the basements of our parents' townhouses. We betrayed
each other often without even knowing it. We broke
promises. We formed the habit of divorce. We talked
about donating lifetimes to the poor masses, but we were
stingy with the afternoons we spent with our kid brothers,
our teenage daughters, or our abandoned parents. We
each went our own way. We became private heroes, tough
loners, pure because untouched. Old systems, structures,
institutions of government, the corporation and the church
had nothing to fear from *our* purity because the "idealistic"
vision with which we began our assault on them became
in the end the ground for our assault on each other. And
we were scattered.

Jesus alludes to only one consequence of the scattering
he predicts—that he himself *will be alone.* Of course, the
words are remembered by John as having been spoken
on the night before he died. At that moment Jesus is seeing
his friends scatter, watching *them* take off, excuse, betray,
be busy, distance themselves with philosophy. The line is
a protest, a memory of Jesus' own fragile manhood:
*Leaving me alone. I do not want to be alone. Loneliness
terrifies.*

It terrifies all of us. Most of the good that we do, at
our desks, on our streets, in our kitchens, is all a flight from
loneliness. Sin, on the contrary, is our perverse "pursuit of
loneliness," to use Philip Slater's words. Sin is that followed urge to leave before the thing is over, to get away
from the crowd whose members are everyone. We find
it so natural to move continually toward the margins of
our communities. And though we do it in the name of

happiness or freedom or independence or integrity, we
end, as often as not, deeply alien to ourselves as well as
to those others we have shunned. Such fear. Such foolishness. The pursuit of loneliness, the flight from intimacy,
friendship and moral and political responsibility, is finally
a form of death of the self. A form of self-killing. The fear
is that community will not be worth the price it exacts
on our freedom; and so, in a million subtle ways, we reject
it and thereby begin the slow death of loneliness that is
far worse than the ordinary pain of living with others. So
it goes with marriage, neighborhood, apartment house,
political party, religious order, and—in and through it all
—the relationship each of us has with God.

Our dread aloneness is so visible in our eyes and so
pervasive in our social structures that it has almost become
the *basis* for what community we can still have with
each other. We share the same deepest fear—that we
are by ourselves, single, in the corner, alone. We *all* look
for ways to have it otherwise.

Jesus speaks his words from a heart which even as he
speaks is already finally and radically alone. The others
are already scattered and he knows it. But he goes on
with other words, saying, *but not really alone.*

How is it possible to be alone but not really alone? How
can you be abandoned but still included in the circle of
friendship? Is this another of those Bible tricks, more of
the mystery-magic in which, as the preachers are always
telling us, everything looks dreary but "salvation" is at
hand? I have to proceed carefully in what I want to say at
this point; I want neither to blot out the critical mind that
makes belief difficult, nor to embrace the cynicism that
makes belief impossible.

Jesus is claiming something for himself. He is *alone, but not really alone.* He is alone, but has a way to live with it. He discovers in himself a way to stand abandoned, but *to stand.* He claims to have a sense of company that survives the loss of all his friends. Why? How? *Because* he says, *the Father is with me.* There it is. *Because the Father is with me. That* is the difference between Jesus and me. He and I may in fact share hearts of chaos, loss of old ideas, confusion about meanings and purposes. But he does not rest in such grim circumstance. Certainly he does not embrace it. He claims to be on to something. He speaks words about it. He displays something that, if it exists in me at all, lies far back, beyond the silences in my life.

Jesus—how else to say it?—believes in God. Jesus lives with God. He is the one who does. I do not. My friends do not. *Not really alone,* he claims. It is the ultimate claim Jesus makes. I will know, he says, the deepest, saddest loss of love possible. I will be betrayed by all those I have chosen. I will bend my body over emptiness. I will go to the edge of it, but I will come back. *I will be alone, but not really alone.* I am no solitary hero, no lone ranger. There will be a listener to whom I will not need to speak. There will be company on the climb. It will keep me going, hold me up. It will make me different from you. And it will give me something to give you.

I give you my loneliness, he says. It makes yours no easier than mine, but full of a meaning you have no right to expect. Our loneliness is what we have in common, what makes us friends. It kills me as it kills you, but if you listen to what I give you, it will tell you something new about God.

It was on a hot desert afternoon that I learned something new about God's loneliness. I had heard stories about a hermit, an Orthodox monk, who lived in a cave —by God, in a cave!—in the Judean hills. He was, they told me, a member of a Greek monastic community whose senior members were allowed the privilege, as they regarded it, of living the hermit's life apart from the monastery. I was told to visit the monastery in the valley and ask permission to visit the hermit. The monks would point the way. I hitchhiked down the desert road to the crumbling, baked-mud compound. The monk who greeted me had the strange, half-crazy look of the guardian monks at the tomb of Christ, black robes, hair everywhere, long fingernails, body odor. In hesitant English he warned me, "You may visit, but Father Jacob will not know you."

"I will be brief," I said.

"Carry this to him, if you please."

He handed me a canvas sack that held oranges and goat's cheese and several bottles of water.

"Surely," I said and set off. Why was I doing this, I wondered, as I followed the faint path into the hills? What was there about the tales of hermits that intrigued me so? I laughed to think of the jokes and the *New Yorker*-style cartoons that represented most of what I knew and thought about the strange people whose calling or compulsion cut them off from almost all human contact. I imagined myself asking, "What is the secret of fulfillment?" and the old man replying, "An active sex life."

But it was no joke. By then I had experienced for myself the pull of the desert, a seductive power that had made solitaries of thousands of human beings. Yes, it could all be simple escapism, flight from responsibility, from confusion, from intimacy. It could be the perverse world-hatred that the world always claims such solitude is. It could be a mental health problem, a cop-out, a lie.

But it could also be the most daring kind of adventure. A life of staring down one's own devils. A life stripped to the barest of human experiences; breathing, eating, drinking, watching the sun move, hearing wind, thinking, sleeping, praying the psalms. Me? I admit to both cynicism and curiosity, but neither of them would have led me to the cave. The mystery of aloneness and what it is in a human life is what drew me. *My* aloneness, and the aloneness of countless men and women who lived in the packed apartments and crowded streets of Boston. Was the aloneness of hermits different than that?

What I saw when I finally came to Father Jacob's cave was a bony old man in black robes and a Greek monk's hat. I was struck immediately that even here in a cave on a mountain ten miles from his desert monastery the man would wear his formal, if tattered, religious garb. But then, I thought, what else?

"Hello," I said. When he heard me he shuffled to his feet and grinned. Most of his teeth were gone.

"I have brought you food." I handed him the bag. He took it and immediately opened it. He pulled out an orange and began peeling it, at the same time motioning me to a stool. I sat. He sat on the floor of the cave and peeled and ate the orange. He offered me nothing. Of course, I thought to myself, I wouldn't have accepted.

The view from the cave was magnificent, overlooking Jericho in the distance; farther out, one could see the

Jordan River and the border with the nation Jordan. I could make out the traces of barbed wire frontiers, and here and there were low concrete lookout bunkers. I thought of the hermit sitting on the stool in his cave and watching the battles of Israel with her Arab neighbors. Did he have any idea of what the mutilated bodies of soldiers looked like? Could he hear their screams? Did he even know what the smoke from tank-cannon was?

When I looked again at the monk, he was grinning at me. He had finished the orange and was nodding.

I said, "Do you speak English?" He only nodded. "*Français?*" I asked. He continued grinning, his head bobbing up and down. Twelve years of hermit life, they had told me. Twelve years can do a number on you, I thought. I was beginning to wonder if he were crazy, with his grinning and nodding.

I tried to hold his eyes in mine, but he was looking me up and down, touching me, almost tasting me with his sight. I began to understand how agitated he was, how disturbed, and how much I might be intruding on him. His eyes darted and flashed until, all at once, they stopped, snapped still, and connected fiercely with my own. I was shocked to find myself so deeply looked into. I wanted to turn my face from his but couldn't. Never in my life had I exchanged such a look with a human being. Our gaze at each other was animal-like in intensity, the sort of *seeing* and *knowing* that creatures who have no words with each other must develop. We were caught deer, beasts on the hunt, breathing and looking, one with our eyes.

Strangely, I do not remember the color of his eyes, nor could I say what I saw looking into them. I do not re-

member how long we held that gaze, but it was not a
stare. Although I barely remember leaving the cave, I
know that we never touched, and he never spoke or stopped
grinning. But I do know some things. He was not crazy,
or I am. He lives in a world that is at the very center
of the same world I live in. Both the burden of life and
the exquisite grace of it are well known to him. And his
eyes enable him to be part of what he sees. I suspect he
knows what war is and what Palestinian refugees in distant camps are suffering and what citrus trees do in their
enchantment of water into fruit and even what his fellow
hermits of Manhattan carry secretly in *their* hearts. I
met the man, learned nothing, but saw nearly everything.
And I saw him seeing as much in me. It is probably a
mark of my old naiveté, but since that afternoon that
toothless, grinning monk remains with me as an image
of the loneliness of God.

The word "God," after all, is a kind of shorthand for
the beyond to which human experience points. I don't
know "God," own "God," or carry "God" in my pocket.
What I do know is that there is a power in existence
itself, in *my* existence, that I am unable to account for
and before which I can do nothing but submit.

There are moments when a human being *understands*
that he is alone, yet alive and longing for communion,
moments when he comes face to face with the loneliness
that is at the heart of existence. Not the banal loneliness
that afflicts us when we are in strange cities, cut off from
our families and friends, but the fearful gulf we discover
precisely in the midst of the acts of love that we share
with friends, spouses, colleagues. This radical loneliness
coexists with deep and rich friendships, the care of good

parents, the love of children, or the faithful tending of communities that struggle on in difficult days.

I am among the fortunate ones, for I carry the tested love of several good people with me everywhere, but I also know those moments that break through the fabric of friendship and strip us naked. Moments when our eyes are locked in the animal gaze of the world and we are forced to realize that human life is life alone. Moments, for example, when conscience wrenches from us a choice we had hoped to avoid. I remember talking to an American Jew in 1973, during the early days of the Yom Kippur war. He had long since stopped thinking of himself as a religious man, and would have described himself as an agnostic. He had built a successful family and professional life that had its own momentum and deep satisfactions. Everything was fine. But when the war broke out and when, as many thought for a time, it looked as though Israel might lose, this Jew was stunned into a turmoil of conscience he had never known before. As a man of the left, he had criticized Israeli militarism and sympathized with the plight of Palestinian Arabs. He had rejected the Arab-baiting that some of his acquaintances indulged in as another example of racism. But when it became necessary to imagine that Israel might be defeated, might even be obliterated and destroyed as a nation, my friend became a changed person.

"I had no way to understand what happened in me," he said. "I didn't sleep for days. When a Zionist group asked for my signature for an ad, I said 'no.' It was so violent, what they wanted to say. But I discovered what I had forgotten: those Jews were my people. I had to do *something*. I thought of flying to Israel just to be there.

But that was foolish. In the end I did nothing. But squirm.
But cry. They were my people. I was gone from them.
But I *had* to see that they survived."

"Now this is what is strange," he said quietly. "I think
I met God in that experience." And then my friend fell
silent.

My friend's story seems to support my earlier description
of the word "God" as a kind of shorthand for the beyond
to which human experience points. The openings to that
beyond occur in the midst of the wrenching conflicts in
which we understand how fragile the act of existence is.
Moments of conscience. Of choice. Even of intimacy. Of
responsibility for another person, for one's people, for
oneself. And though those moments may be profoundly
concerned with community and identification with others,
their burden is born by persons utterly alone.

Human aloneness is a kind of shorthand for the aloneness of God. God is one. One only. Lonely. The Solitude
of Solitude. *But,* as Jesus says, *not really alone.* God is
God's own company. God is friendship to himself in such
a way that the burden of existence, which my Jewish
friend described, does not destroy life but opens it to
new levels. God's aloneness opens him to new levels of
his own existence. Perhaps this is what traditional Christian language about *trinity* struggles to express. At the
very heart of solitude there is companionship, as in the
core of companionship there is loneliness. Perhaps that is
what I saw in the hermit's eyes.

It is this continual opening from loneliness to communion and from communion to loneliness that is revealed to us when we are in touch with our act of existence
itself. That opening, that movement, that flow is the act

of life. The pursuit of loneliness is the self-destructive will to close the opening, to stop the flow, to refuse to go beyond aloneness to its center, which is communion. The pursuit of loneliness is suicide. "God" is the word we use to describe the opposite of suicide, the structure of life that keeps life going. God keeps life alive. God keeps existence in being, even through the wrenching of conscience and the loss of sleep. God is what a hermit discovers in himself when, gazing on war in the valley, refugees in the plain, or into the eyes of an awkward visitor, he discovers that though he thought he was alone, he was not really alone at all.

I have told you all this so that you may have peace in me. There *is* a kind of peace in knowing that Jesus was lonely. A kind of peace in imagining that God is lonely. In knowing that everyone is—even the perfect, cool, controlled American males who claim nothing but conquest. There is a kind of peace that comes of sounding your own depths —even if they prove to be bottomless and therefore awful. Bottomless is not the same as empty. There is a kind of peace in facing one's loneliness squarely.

But the peace Jesus offers is not a stoic, tight-lipped courage. Jesus tells us he is alone so that we can understand he is one of us. And he tells us he is not really alone so that we can understand he is one of God. He offers himself as our shorthand. If we *can* call him "brother" and therefore have a way to speak about ourselves, and if we *can* call him "God" and therefore have a way to speak about the beyond in our midst, there is peace in that. It is a matter of knowing you need to be saved. And of knowing from what. And by whom.

I think, however, of my Jewish friend, who still shares his burden with his people; of Palestinians who lose everything daily; and of myself, moving uncertainly between belief and non-belief. Not much *peace* that I see in any of it. But is this Jesus' failure or ours? I turn his memory over and wrap it in the claims of my people, of my times, of my solitude. What happens is not peace. What happens is we *cling,* we hang on. We hold fast, we do not make sense.

But neither do we kill ourselves. God is not comfort, but the opposite of suicide. Perhaps *peace* becomes the act of living when there are good reasons not to. *Peace* may be living in the knowledge of the good possibilities that remain, even for war-weary people. It is important that there is a way to be *alone, but not really alone.*

By the time I came to these thoughts, I realized that something had changed in my expectations of "belief." It may have been the effect of weeks spent in the monk's room, or of the silence of the desert, or of the picture of Jesus that grows on you when you read John on a hill halfway between Bethlehem and Jerusalem. But by then the "belief" I was trying to claim no longer promised holiness or prayerfulness or comfort or docility or even religion. What I found myself talking about, thinking about, and laying at God's feet was *trouble.*

In the world you will have trouble. That's the truth, and I knew it. The "belief" that had embarrassed me and from which I was in flight was, I began to understand, a kind of idolatry that tried to use religion as a shield from trouble. The Jesus-idolators—with their buttons, rock music, and good looks, their holy orders, pressed robes, and Chi-Rho cuff links of gold—they held that being God meant no loneliness, no hassles, no thoughts about doing oneself in, no trouble. Jesus says, "I am alone. You will be." Jesus says, "I got troubles. So do you."

I got trouble. It keeps me up at night. I go to restaurants, bars, and strange cities, not running away from it but looking for its name. I got troubles. I don't know yet what they are. I have a cancer of something not my body. Partly it's the times, growing up loving the Air Force, and losing not only the war in Asia but also one's sense of nobility and purpose. Blood still drips from roots that were cut that day I went to the Pentagon not as a worshipper to a shrine but as one of a massive jury bearing the verdict, "Guilty." Such are the troubles that have stunned us from our optimism, and even now invite guilty paralysis instead of a genuine conversion of politics and humanity; that make us all Irish teenagers, slayers and victims both; African freedom fighters whose leaders are slain or bought; prison guards who are locked into hatreds and fears; children who are the weapons and pawns of racist parents. And there are troubles hidden in silos waiting to make everything else seem good by comparison with the last grim day they promise all of us.

Trouble—partly, it's personal, private. It is wanting desperately to be a faithful friend to just a few people, but surrendering again and again to the loss of nerve that comes disguised as selfishness. Partly, it's the wages one pays for the habit of cynicism, a habit which makes it impossible to separate authentic criticism from the willful loss of faith. Partly it's our lack of humor. Partly it's the sexual neurosis of our time, which collects its tribute in prolonged adolescence. It's even poetry, which takes its pound of flesh in the best hours of one's life. Troubles.

Yes. Right. I have them. So do you. *In the world,* Jesus says, *you will.*

Trouble, we might say, is therefore a sign of the presence of God. If trouble doesn't mean God is there, the absence of trouble means he isn't. *Do you believe at last?* Jesus says. *Then you got trouble. That* promise comes true. *That* connection makes me want to reclaim belief. Almost as if he had said: "Do you believe at last? Then you've lost your faith. Do you believe at last? Your folks won't like you. Do you believe at last? You'll go to jail. You'll lose your nerve. Do you believe at last? You will get up from your bed at night looking for someone to talk to."

Jesus says, "God is with me and I'm in trouble. What do you want?" Jesus faces trouble, steers into it; he can freely take it on because he has this sense deep in the core of his selfhood that, though alone, he is not alone. The Companion in whom he has his being is with him. No trouble can change that. So, no trouble paralyzes. No trouble turns him into a liar, a grabber, a son of a bitch. What is his resource, his strength, his heart that is flesh and iron at once? "You think I like crucifixion? Am I crazy? But what I have to do, I do. I will stand on those nails. They will know they had a man by the bone. I believe in God."

Jesus had exactly that sense we lack and long for. He looked to his own inner deep and saw something. We see the darkness with which we exchange the animal stare. He listened to himself, to the claims of his people; he listened and heard the word of truth. We listen and it is either too loud or too quiet. If that One in whom we have our being is with us, he does not say anything we understand. He does not show himself.

That is how I know I am Jim, not Jesus (though we share initials and parents' names). And that is how I know the memory of Jesus is important to me. I turn it over in my mind. I look at it and *there* at least I see something. I listen and *there* I hear. I need more than I have. If what the memory says to me is true, I need Jesus.

Be brave, he says. I am trying. Sometimes my lower lip quivers and I am six years old, stuck in the big rain drainage tunnel by the garage. I am ready to let go, to bawl, to shake, to give myself up for dead. No Mom here. No Dad. No help. When you're stuck in the tunnel by yourself, you understand. You learn. Later, you remember. *Be brave?* Now and most times, I am. And so are you. We *do* squirm toward the light. We *do* get out. We *do* stand up, if not on nails, on earth which is its own pain, its own reward. We *do* return to the promises our lives made. We make further promises. We go home. We try again to love them all, Mom, Dad, brothers, sisters, friends. We do not give in to death. We do not grab. We do not go to war.

We listen to our times, to our people, to the pleas of the throng, and to our own cracked silence. We hear no words of sense, no new names for God, no ways to pray or stop the marchers from killing each other. No hint of rain for the dying earth. But we listen, crawling further into silence and into Babel. There is no Mom, no Dad, no magic, no answer. But neither is there reason to think that the Word is gone forever. Why should death have its way this time?

I watch the sunset and see the eyes of a stunned deer, a hermit, a Jew. Such hurting. Such knowledge. My left eye burns, but I look for a long time, without staring.

Caught on this small piece of earth, I am here to be its eyes and ears, to crawl deeper into it. To stand on it alive.

Be brave, Jesus says, *I have conquered the world.* One word of truth outweighs the world. If so, it outweighs me, my burden of lies. If so, he has conquered me, my darkness, my silence, my lack of nerve. Because *I* am the world. *I* am disbelief. *I* am selfishness. *I* am scattering itself. *I* am the love of loneliness.

I turn him over in my mind, not claiming to be an ally. Not presuming to be his servant. Not wanting to be his spokesman. I turn his memory over in my mind, listening to his silence, seeing his darkness but still hoping to be his willing victim.

PART TWO
Recovery

‖ 4 ‖

Abba: Dear Folks

About halfway through that summer on a monks' hill in Israel, it began to be clear to me that, despite my mornings in the desert and my adventures in the shrines of the Land and my late-night journeys to Abu's bar, I was not going to be changed in personality or belief in any dramatic fashion. I had hoped, I suppose, to be knocked from a horse into certainty, one way or the other. Perhaps even expected to meet God face to face. Visiting in Israel did help me *imagine* Jesus and his people much more clearly than I ever had before. I went to the Sea of Galilee and *saw* places they had seen, swam in water Peter had tried to walk on, slept on a beach that might have been the scene of a charcoal fire and the sharing of some fish and bread among them. But in the last analysis the Sea of Galilee is just another lovely lake, remarkable then because it was in the shadow of the Golan Heights, on which a war was being waged. I finally had to accept the fact that, for all my silence, solitude, and study of the Book, I was still going to be a stranger to God.

I could now feel in my bones what I had heard and said before, but was coming to understand only in reading John—that God is unknowable. "The world has not known you" (John 17:25). "No one has ever seen God" (1:18). "You have never heard his voice, you have never seen his shape and his words find no home in you" (5:37).

Curiously enough, Jesus did not seem to identify belief with *knowing* God at all. In fact he mercilessly rebuked people who casually claimed to be on intimate terms with God. Though he remained an observant Jew, he repudiated those contemporary forms of piety that promised automatic access to God. He was in revolt, I began to see, against "prayer" as it was understood and practiced in his day. As he said to the woman at the well: "The hour is coming when you will worship the Father neither on this mountain [the holy place of Samaria] nor in Jerusalem. God is spirit and those who worship must worship in spirit and in truth" (4:19-24).

"You think you own God?" he might have said. "You have his photograph hanging on the walls of your temples?" Not even Israel knows God! God is spirit. God is wind. "Wind blows wherever it wants to" (3:8).

So I sit here on the stone wall around the house of prayer on the hill between birth and death. The wind blows from the sea forty miles to the west. It blows through my hair, over my body, and on to the desert, toward the ruins of Herod's castle, and beyond to the border, where soldiers listen to it for the sounds of war. You can hear the wind, but that's all you know of it. You can see it swishing through the willows and pushing clouds. But it does not speak or stop to sit with you. The wind has its own business. No one knows its story. It is secret to itself.

God is wind. Silent as wind. If, as John suggests, God is unknowable, then perhaps I was not a failed believer, an atheist, or a fool because I did not know him. It is easy to strike a false note of anxiety when describing what can only be called the *absence* of God, especially when it may be, as John *almost* says, that God is one who by definition must seem absent. If one experiences only silence from God, it may be that God is silence itself. So, at least, it seems to me, sitting here on the stone wall. There is only wind, no whispers, just wind.

I think of that line from the Christmas Mass, remembered from my boyhood treks to church at midnight, the hour of the earth's pause in its turning: "When a great silence settled over the whole world, the eternal Word of God leapt down from its heavenly throne." When John says, as he alone does, that Jesus is the *Word* of God, he hints that Silence Itself seeks to be expressed and known. God is silent and unknowable to his creatures, but somehow God is as restless in that silence as we are.

"Jesus is the Word with which God has broken his silence," says Joachim Jeremias (*The Central Message of the New Testament* [Scribners, 1965], p. 90). John argues that in Jesus God ends the silent treatment. Not that the silence is over, but that in Jesus, one of us hears. In Jesus, one of us knows. If that is so, the relationship with Jesus is crucial, because in him God is knowable. The silence has a Word about itself. "He alone has seen the Father" (John 6:46). As John reminds us, whoever believes in Jesus has eternal life, and "eternal life is this, to know you as the only true God" (17:3).

So now the problem settles exactly on Jesus, on "believing in him." And how does one do that? Is there another way than by turning his memory over in one's mind like a lost coin? By searching out his meaning in the memory of one's people? But even here John suggests something unexpected: the Word of God is not merely the Word—"The Word was made flesh and lived with us" (1:14).

Flesh! John's use of this expression is a scandal to the pious. It describes human beings precisely in contrast to God by pointing to their frailty, mortality, and tendency to get it wrong. Flesh—"It is the strongest expression of contempt for human existence" (Jeremiah, *Central Message,* p. 87). Flesh is what religious people perennially reject, flee from, denounce. And now I am in flight from them. I know my flesh and my flesh knows me. It opens up the hole in my head precisely with its dread silence, its forgetfulness of God's name, its ignorance of what it needs most to know.

But when this Word becomes flesh, there is no contempt, no put-down, no accusation. When this Word becomes flesh, John says, "We behold its glory" (1:14). Its beauty, its grandeur. We *see.* And not only the fragile and delicate lines of the naked body. We see in the flesh all we need to know of God. Learn God by learning Jesus. Learn Jesus by embracing the flesh of oneself and others.

Prayer becomes possible when we remember that it is not the opposite of flesh, but its glorification. Whatever communion with God is, it is at least this—an offering of one's flesh, one's real experience. Worship in "spirit and truth" is at once worship in flesh and silence. This sort of worship, this sort of prayer, begins, as I do, with the admission that we do not know exactly who God is, do not know exactly what to say to him, do have something else to do, and, on most days, would rather do it.

There is silence and flesh about Jesus. And on this night he does have something else to do, but he would rather not do it—he is going to his death. But now I am listening to Jesus in the prayer he speaks in the seventeenth chapter of John. My memory of him has come down to these words, this plea, this last gift to his friends. It is his wish for them. It is his last testament, his will. It is the summary of his message and meaning. I am listening to it because my time in Israel, my search for the old faith, my movement toward recovery, all bring me to this last moment of his. I want to reread this prayer of his and study it and make it mine. I want to take this prayer of his and pray it.

Father, the hour has come; glorify your Son so that your Son may glorify you. And through the power over all mankind that you have given him let him give eternal life to all those you have entrusted to him. And eternal life is this: to know you the only true God and Jesus Christ whom you have sent. I have glorified you on earth and finished the work that you gave me to do. Now, Father, it is time for you to glorify me with that glory I had with you before ever the world was. (John 17:1-5)

The fact that Jesus calls God "Father" is so familiar to us that it is hard to appreciate what an outrageous and disturbing and, I suspect, attractive man it made Jesus to those who heard him. If the language of Jesus grows stale for us, it may be because it has been so domesticated by our usage that it is no longer provocative to us as it must have been to his first hearers. Today, when the sexist structures of language itself are being challenged, perhaps the problematic character of Jesus' use of the term "Father" will resurface as feminists and others call into question the exclusively male character of official God-language. Nevertheless, Jesus' address of God in this fashion was such a liberating cry that it had to be somewhat scandalous. Though Israel did claim the right to speak of God as Father of the People, it did so only fourteen times in the Jewish Scriptures. That an individual person should claim such a relationship was quite literally unthinkable. "There is no evidence so far that in Palestinian Judaism of the first millennium anyone addressed God as 'my father.' But Jesus did just this. . . . Not only do the four gospels attest that Jesus used this address, but they report unanimously that he did so in all his prayers" (Jeremias, *Central Message,* p. 16).

How did Jesus come to this? What did it mean to him? Perhaps by paying attention to the struggles in the flesh of our own lives we might understand what this extraordinary experience might have been to Jesus. As we sound the depths of the inner reaches of consciousness, as we pass through the stillness to the discovery of the Word, as we move with hearts haunted by nothingness to some faint hints of a presence we cannot name, as we grow up and learn who we are, we may approximate Jesus' growing in wisdom and in grace.

It seems clear that Jesus continually took the measureless measure of himself. Echoes. False signals. Silence. Confusions. But somehow, at some point, he discovered this vast communion, this Presence in himself, and he knew it was of God. And, therefore, so was he. Jesus experienced God in himself, as surely as in myself I experience shadows. Neither theology nor dogma nor tradition provided a solution. Jesus discovered union between himself and God. In his time and place, a patriarchal society—he would surely have chosen the feminine address in a matriarchal one—the only human experience, the only word available to him to describe the support, the life-source, the nurture, the love he discovered in himself, was *"Abba," "Father."*

"There is no doubt that the *Abba* which Jesus uses to address God reveals the very basis of his communion with God" (Jeremias, *Central Message,* p. 21). It has something to do with parenthood. It has something to do with the *Abba* in *my* life. Mom, Pop, the ones I carry in my heart and in whom I am carried. *Abba* can be taken and, in our heightened consciousness about the violence of sexist language, *should* be taken to refer to that primordial communion the child experiences with the parent, either or both.

In my case, both. I do not have a continual communion with the tender, nurturing, challenging life that got me this far, whether of God or of my mom and dad. But there are moments when my relationship with that gift of life, focused in that man and woman, is utterly unambiguous, a joy, a surpassing peace. Moments that I remember in trying to understand what this word *Abba* is to Jesus. (Ah yes, he's turned thirty; one does soften toward the old folks then.)

I think of waking up on dark winter mornings to my mother's sharp voice: "Get up! Up! Get it up!" And then four minutes later: "I said, get up! You'll be late!" And I know that even now the temptation to stay in bed, which precedes the temptation to sleep forever, to roll over, to refuse the day, is still as powerful in me as it was on those cold days when I hated the thought of school. Now that the stakes are higher and the question is whether I will *live* or not, that calling voice of my mother still has its effect. I *do* get up. I *do* seize the day. I *do* accept responsibility for a piece of the earth for a portion of time. But it's more than me doing it. Left to myself I'd have overdosed on sleep or its equivalent long ago. When I was a boy Mom refused to leave me to myself. She shook me, challenged me, called me. I responded. I formed the habit of getting up, of going out, of living. I took, and continue to take, her calling with me. It is one of the ways she lives with me still. There is an *Abba* for me in that, a basis for my communion with what is beyond me, calling, demanding, coaxing, encouraging. It is not only that my mother taught me but that she remains with me still in this, though it is years since I heard those words or their like from her. I am flesh of her flesh.

I am flesh of her Chicago girlhood, the time when *she* learned to go boldly into the day, though there were reasons not to. I remember when we first visited the old house where she grew up in St. Gabriel's parish on the South Side. I remember the weathered grey porch, the floating stairs, the big kitchen, the curtains—not doors— that separated rooms. A big house for a big family. Eight children. Depression years that called *her* out of childhood into working to help provide the food for the other kids. I remember walking into that house in my boyhood and knowing I'd been there before. I had always been there. It was *Mom's* place. It was mine.

My mother was a teen-age telephone operator. She did what she had to do. First, to help with the bills at home; later, to help my dad go to law school at night. She has this way of calling the best out of the people she loves, not pushing, not forcing. Inviting. When the call comes, you know two things: you have to do it, and you can. I am not talking about the shove toward "achievement," though surely that's there, but about the fundamental sense she gives her loved ones that they are loved and therefore responsible. My dad built a lifetime out of his response to her strong calling. My brothers and I began lifetimes believing in ourselves because she did.

When the moment came to leave home, to say farewell, to let go of each other, more or less, we were all ready. Not that it was easy, or that we were exempt from the hurting or the anger or the loss or the misunderstanding or the temporary madness. But the moment of that last embrace at the door found us prepared to leave the sleep of childhood. "Goodbye." "Goodbye." Such hurting. Such comfort. Now, when I visit home, we reenact the farewell. My mother's lifetime of faithful love that is its own act of sacrifice—not martyrdom—makes our moments of farewell not the neurotic scenes of abandonment one might fear, but moments when she sends us forth into the day, into *our* lives. Hurting, because there is the loss of yesterday's innocence for all of us. Comforted, because we carry each other in our hearts. *Abba.* I am flesh of her flesh.

As for my dad and me, that's quite a story. He reached the peak of his life as an Air Force general, a powerful, accomplished, dedicated man whose idealism and commitment took shape in a world of intrigue and barely balanced terror that was just ending when I grew up. The rite of passage that made me an adult was celebrated at the main gate of Hanscom Air Force Base. It was my confirmation, my coming of age, my first arrest. We were sitting in the street, attempting to block the way of trucks that carried components for the electronic bombing systems that were being used with deadly effect in Vietnam. I remember the Air Force policeman pointing at me, saying, "Him, start with him!" I was completely limp, but when they picked me up I knew that something had broken inside me. It was an immensely sad moment. Yet I also knew that I had come to it straight from the man who had prepared me for manhood. I did not tell my dad about my arrest, but he knew. There was between us the heavy silence wars often lay over families. I was silence of his silence. Perhaps the *Abba* implies a distance and a wordlessness and an estrangement that are as real and powerful as the intimacy and nurture and support. But certainly the *Abba* implies the primacy of the latter. Word does have its way over silence. And between me and my dad, affection does have its way over estrangement.

Dear Pop, I remember the last time I reached to you. It was only last month when I came home. We were both at the kitchen table and you caught both my hands, so to speak, in yours. You turned them into fists and boxed with me playfully. About Nixon, I think, who finally makes us both laugh. And I knew again there are adventures and dares and braveries in me enough to live several lives in difficult times, happily. That's how I always feel when your fondness for me shows.

There is silence and flesh between me and what is precious to me. The silence and the flesh separate us, keep us apart with wordlessness and urges and lost memories. In the silence, I sit with my mother over coffee, unable to move, understanding the loneliness of a parent whose children are gone. In the flesh, I watch my father hit a golf ball perfectly, effortlessly, one putt from the cup; then I step to the tee and attack the small white sphere as if it held all the demons of the world. And like all the demons in the world, it refuses to be moved—and I miss.

But the silence and the flesh still hold us in a fragile act of union. In the flesh, my father has a peculiar way of coughing that is like no one else. I cough that way myself just now and know again whose son I am. In the silence we return to the old house and understand that a past like ours is a promise with its own future. The whole exploding act of life, beginning at the beginning, breaks out in simple acts expressing fondness between human beings. We know we are made for something wonderful. We know there are possibilities beyond our imagining. We know we are capable of more than we have yet dared. When I touch this fondness, this challenge of flesh to flesh, this embrace, I could almost call it God. I almost understand when Jesus does.

The notion of God as *Abba* grew increasingly important to the first Christians. As the century wore on it became practically the exclusive form of address used for God. (In the earliest Gospel, Mark, Jesus uses it only three times. In John, he uses it one hundred times.) When John seizes upon the notion of *Abba* to characterize Jesus' relationship with God, he does so as a way of emphasizing the uniqueness of Jesus. For all the ways we might discover the *Abba* within ourselves, it remains true that no one experiences the kind of familiarity and intimacy with God that Jesus claims. Indeed, even with one's own parents the moments of fondness and communion occur in the context of a pervasive tension that includes misunderstanding and resentment.

Because *Abba* represents the center of Jesus' awareness of himself and the world, he alone claims to have broken through the ambivalent and inconsistent experience human beings have of life. Not that he is exempt from mistrust, but that he breaks through it. For all the power of good parents' love, none of us is spared the self-doubt that is passed on infallibly from generation to generation. We are born with a constitutional inability to relax in the gift of love. We are not that sure of being accepted, acceptable. We are always wondering why they are looking at us like that (Mom, Dad, the passing policeman). The lack of certainty on this point makes the moments of fondness a great joy. But it also makes those moments of indecisiveness and loneliness a source of paralysis.

Jesus was not paralyzed. At some point in his life, probably about age thirty, he taps a well, he finds out who he is, he discovers his mission. The word he uses for all of this is *Abba*. It is one of the only things we know with certainty about the man Jesus. "Here we see who the historical Jesus was: the man who had the power to address God as *Abba*. It is *ipsissima vox*" (Jeremias, *Central Message*, p. 30).

Abba, the hour has come. Glorify your Son. Now, Abba! This prayer that Jesus prays the night before he dies reveals that it is precisely into this relationship of intimacy, consistency, and unambivalent, positive regard that Jesus invites his followers. Already, in giving the Lord's Prayer,

Jesus has made the address *Abba* the token of discipleship. His friends are the ones who claim this kind of intimacy with God. They do not discover it in themselves until they learn what it is like by listening to and looking at Jesus. But once the name is given and the Word is spoken, and the faint echo of that intimacy is heard in one's own hidden places, everything shifts ever so slightly. Just enough to make a difference. It is like what happens between grown people when they discover that the bonds of childhood and parenthood have not been broken by time as they had feared, but have changed and, in a way, deepened and strengthened. It is like what happened in me the day I could take my *Abba,* Mom and Pop, into my arms, having learned to be a man and a son both.

‖ 5 ‖

World Too Much With Us

I have made your name known to men you took from the world to give me. They were yours and you gave them to me and they have kept your word. Now at last they know that all you have given me comes indeed from you; and they have believed that it was you who sent me. I pray for them. I am not praying for the world but for those you have given me. [John 17:6-9]

When you sit on the highest hill for miles around, on the edge of Judea's desert, looking down on Jerusalem, Bethlehem, the borders of war, the ruins of the past, and roads that lead unbroken to the horizon, you begin to think you are looking at the "world" itself. I imagined Jesus sitting on such a hill, watching camel caravans pass with their rich goods from the East, watching nomadic tribes war with each other, watching pilgrims going up to Mount Moriah. The scene suggested a sense of the vast web of life, space, history, sorrow, and conflict that he referred to as "the world."

As John remembers it, the word "world" was a key one for Jesus. It also is for us; we are movers, the mobile ones, travelers, pilgrims, tourists. We go from place to place, equally at home or not at home, nearly everywhere. We learn from television and reading that the world itself is our village. So it was for me, born in the American Midwest, raised in cities of the East and South, schooled in Europe, settled for the moment in New England, and, by the time of these reflections, a visiting stranger in Israel, where I was as much at home as anywhere.

Jesus prays for his friends, but *not for the world* (John 17:9). He is *not in the world any longer, but they are in the world* (17:11). *The world hated them because they belong to the world no more than I belong to the world* (17:14). He does not ask the Father *to remove them from the world, but to protect them from the Evil One* (17:15). As the Father sent Jesus, so has he sent his friends *into the world* (17:18), *that the world might believe . . . realize* (17:21). *The world has not known* the Father. Only Jesus has and those to whom Jesus has revealed him (17:25).

What is this "world" Jesus talks about? Clearly, the way he uses it in these passages, the word refers to something other than the Rand-McNally globe. Something other than the vistas one sees from a hill in Israel or from the window of a 707. There is a vehemence Jesus displays in talking about this "world." Even with pollution and monetary crises and failed governments and ongoing games of musical wars, we find it hard to muster the kind of resentment toward the world that Jesus seems to manifest. And not only resentment but cold fear, if not for himself, for his friends.

I remember enough of my seminary scripture courses

to realize that this language of Jesus has posed problems for people through the centuries. It is easy to distort Jesus' meanings at least as much as a flat map distorts the earth. There is, for example, the long and venerable tradition accepted by many of us called "hating the world." This has usually meant hating whatever feels good, and has, of course, been our way of desiring something so much that we don't dare allow ourselves the experience of it. I am thinking of the ease with which the positive discipline of "mortification" can become an exercise in mere denial and negation. Christian hatred of the world has often taken the form of hatred of the private and pleasurable acts of human existence.

What we tend to forget is that there is always a political dimension to "hating the world." By now we have no excuse for not seeing how "detachment from worldly affairs" can serve to perpetuate the structures of power, even if they are corrupt and oppressive. The sanctification of suffering, usually the suffering of the dispossessed, has all too often been preached—and practiced—in the name of Christianity and other religions, and has earned them the vengeful opposition of the great reform and revolutionary movements of the twentieth century. Revolution and reform apparently begin in the act of refusing to submit to the suffering that results from class stratification or the arbitrary exercise of power.

If it hurts, it's holy; if it feels good, it's a sin. That might almost be the motto for wide areas of Christian practice. It may be difficult to know precisely what Jesus meant by "the world," but we can be certain his words are not intended to underwrite or encourage systems that perpetuate poverty, hunger, and war. We have yet to understand fully what Jesus meant, and so, with rare consistency, we forget that there are several "worlds." We manage usually to hate the wrong one.

As the scholars remind us, it is important to contrast Jesus' negative attitude toward what he calls "the world" in these passages with other, more positive, references in John. "The world" is what God so loved that he sent Jesus "to save it" (3:16-17; 10:36; 12:47) and "to bring full life" to it (4:42; 1 John 4:14). Jesus is "the lamb of God who takes away the sin of the world" (1:29).

In Jesus' experience "the world" becomes increasingly identified with those who turn against him under the leadership of "the Evil One." By the time of his last supper there is understandable anger and hostility in his attitude toward "the world," but by then the expression has a new and narrowed reference. Jesus seems to interpret his coming passion and death as the final struggle between himself and "the Evil One," between his followers and those who were against him. By virtue of his death-glorification-resurrection, however, he "conquered the world" (16:33) and cast down "the Prince of this world" (12:31).

Clearly the contrast Jesus makes is not the temporal or spatial one between earth and heaven, or between blessed suffering and evil pleasure, or between the sacred and the profane. Nor is his contrast a matter of one "group," whether socially, racially, or religiously defined, against another. The contrast is a matter of *choice*. It reaches to the heart of what it means to be a human being, free and responsible. In the context in which Jesus speaks, the crucial choice is the one about himself: Are you for me or against me? In the context of the broader significance of Jesus' life, the crucial choice is the one about your neighbor: Are you for him or against him? "The world" is inhabited by persons who decided against God by deciding against Jesus, by deciding against their neighbors.

In John "the world" is identified—and this is the key insight—with those who condemn themselves (3:19). The choice against the neighbor, against Jesus, is finally a choice of self-destruction. There is no superficial opposition between one's own good and the good of the other. The choice against the other is rooted in the choice against oneself. At this level "the world" takes on the meaning of what might be called "the milieu of self-destruction." Jesus' fear of "the world" is rooted in his clear awareness of how easily one can make the self-destructive choice.

It is interesting to remember that two of the three metaphors used to describe Jesus' experience of temptation by "the Evil One" involved what one could only call temptations to suicide. "If you are the Son of God," the "Evil One" said, "throw yourself down" (Matt. 4:6). From the highest tower of the temple. From the edge of the highest mountain in Judea. I think of those fleeting urges, that came as I jogged across it, to fling myself off the edge of the Massachusetts Avenue Bridge. And I imagine Jesus thinking of jumping, feeling the irrational and evil urge making its way up his throat toward the center of his freedom. In the center of freedom one *knows* that suicide is an option that never allows itself to be closed off finally. I imagine Jesus knowing that, confronting self-destructive forces in himself, knowing their power and fearing them. *I do not ask you to remove them from the world, but to protect them from the Evil One* (John 17:15).

There was a kid in my class in the eighth grade whose father died suddenly, mysteriously. I remember the whispered rumor that he had shot himself. I remember the macabre gossip of the children, of whom I was one: suicide would send you to hell; you couldn't be buried in church ground; to "commit" suicide was to "commit" mortal sin, sin-to-the-death. I didn't know how to talk to or even look at the boy whose father was the subject of our rumors. I remember thinking even then that surely God was not as harsh on suicide as we were, but I had no worked-out reason for thinking so, nor any language with which to express the hope. As I recall, the whole subject made me so uneasy that I began avoiding the boy, who had once been a friend of mine. Today I don't remember his name or even what he looked like.

The second remembered time that suicide was an issue in my life came a few years later. It involved a bachelor friend of my parents who had been in government service with my father and had remained one of my parents' closest friends. He had been like a third parent to me during all my time of growing up. When I made my first communion, he gave me a Bible which I still have. When I was confirmed, I took his name as my sacramental name. He was the only adult whom I addressed by his first name.

One day I noticed the scars on his wrists. I was about fourteen, old enough to see the pool of suffering in his eyes. When I asked my mother about the scars, she reminded me of our visits years before to a spacious old estate in which he was living. She told me that it had been a mental hospital, that he had had a breakdown and that, yes, he had cut his wrists. He had tried to kill himself. I was stunned to think that someone I knew and loved had ever been that desperate, that lonely, that hopeless. By then I had tempered my religious horror at suicide with a primitive kind of psychologizing. Oh, well, I'd say to myself, he wasn't responsible. It wasn't his fault. He couldn't have been punished. He had been "sick." He had been in a hospital, hadn't he? I had gone from the dread theology in which suicide was a mortal sin one "committed" to the dread psychology in which persons who attempted suicide were themselves "committed."

By a kind of strange coincidence, one of the few books I had brought with me to Israel was A. Alvarez's study of suicide, *The Savage God* (Random House, 1972). As I reentered the story of Jesus' life and death, recalled my own past, and touched on some of my present conflicts, I found myself returning again and again to the notion of suicide. Alvarez's study of the poetry of suicide made me remember weeping the winter before at the news that John Berryman had killed himself. He did it by jumping from the Mississippi River Bridge at the University of Minnesota, where as a student I had heard him lecture and had begun to love him. He jumped from the very bridge many of us had crossed on the way to hear him. He had been obsessed by his own death, as the most casual reading of many of his poems reveals. I remembered one line which declared, "We all change our minds halfway down to the river." And I dearly hoped he did.

Alvarez reminded me that "one of the most remarkable features of the arts in this century has been the sudden sharp rise in the casualty rate among artists." Among these official suicides—as opposed to what might be classified as the alcoholic suicides of people like Brendan Behan or Dylan Thomas—are Van Gogh, Virginia Woolf,

Hart Crane, Delmore Schwartz, Cesare Pavese, Paul Celan, Randall Jarrell, Sylvia Plath, Mayakovsky, Yesenin, Modigliani, Gorki, Gertler, Jackson Pollock, Mark Rothko, Ernest Hemingway, Montherlant, and William Inge.

There can, of course, be smugness in identifying one's own pain with the whole of existence, and even great artists are capable of such smugness. It is important not to try to sanctify their deaths. And it would dishonor the memory of such people to romanticize suicide in their names, or to trivialize their suffering by calling it self-sacrificing heroism and therefore somehow unreal. But when many of the very persons who most reveal us to ourselves commit the act of suicide, it is important to ask what *that* might reveal about the world we are building.

This somber preoccupation of mine was compounded during those days when a monk at a monastery where I had visited killed himself shortly after I had left. I do not know if I had met the man. Presumably I prayed with him. I must have sat in chapel with him, watched him, bent over the psalms. When I heard what had happened, that one of these monks had shot himself in the head, it was as if a brother of mine had done it. Or as if I had done it. Monks do not shoot themselves, they do not suffer that kind of desperation, they are not that lonely. Now it was too late to hold him back, to grab him by the hand, to tell him I was sorry for not knowing what burden he carried, for not telling him of mine.

I thought of my dear Paulist brother George, who, only two years before, had died of an overdose of barbiturates. No one could call it suicide; his death remained a mystery of anguish and freedom. But the last time I had seen George we *had* shared our common burden of death and loneliness. We had attended a particularly wrenching and moving play together, one which cut us both and opened us, if only briefly, to each other. I remember standing silently, stiffly, with him in the lobby, during the intermission, drinking orange juice, looking at ourselves and each other in the wall-length mirrors. Finally he said—and for how many, besides himself, was he speaking?—"There are too many ways to kill yourself, all too few to live."

I remember sitting one night with the writer William Gibson as he described the suicide of his friend William Inge, who had struggled through periodic bouts of depression and discouragement. Late one night he called Gibson long-distance to tell him that he was at the breaking point. Gibson listened, tried to tell him to hold on, groped for a word that would lend strength to his friend. But the word didn't come. Finally Gibson said that he would arrange for Inge to get the help he needed, but that it required that he make some other phone calls. "Hold on, Bill," Gibson said, "I'll call you right back." Gibson then contacted the hospital where Inge had received treatment before and arranged for him to be admitted the next morning. He called Inge right back, but there was no answer. When his friend killed himself that night, Gibson himself touched death in a new way. As he told me, "We all carry a death sentence inside ourselves, you know."

Now I think of Paul's words, "We carry death in our bodies" (2 Cor. 4:8). We are born with an urge to ruin what is precious, beginning with ourselves. The power of that urge is revealed in the way that we can so easily and mistakenly perceive the very temptation to self-destruction as romantic, fulfilling, or heroic. In a life where nothing seems noteworthy, the deliberate embrace of death pretends to offer a supreme identity. The cult of suicide depends on a lie: if they won't remember how I lived, they'll remember how I died. There is a profound sanity in seeing through that lie.

To know someone who chooses suicide, to feel the pain of that act out of love for the one who does it, is to recognize the futility and deception that characterizes the death we all carry in our bodies. Hope does not dispel the fear. Even belief does not exempt us from the threat of the despair that overpowers so many. Edward Albee has George ask the question that forms the title of his play, "Who's Afraid of Virginia Woolf?" Who's afraid of the seduction of death that killed that great woman? Who's afraid of the urge to ruin one's most precious gift? Even though one carries death in one's body, as Paul goes on to say, "for the sake of life," even though one chooses to hope, there is always reason enough to be afraid. "Who's afraid of Virginia Woolf?" George's wife, Martha, answers for all of us when she says, "I am, George. I am."

And so, when I turned to Jesus, the words he had spoken almost in fear and trembling about "the world" made me think of suicide. The suicides of strangers, writers, friends, myself. "The world" is the milieu of suicide, the act of self-killing, a metaphor for the vast and nameless forces with which we are all in conflict and which, if they had their way, would leave us alone and dead.

There is the technical meaning of suicide—the ultimate act of physical self-destruction. And there is the broader human meaning that includes many kinds of self-destructive activity that stop short of the violent ending of one's physical life. There are slow forms of self-killing (one thinks of alcoholism) and quick ones (single-car accidents?) which no coroner would record as "suicide." But even the broader human meaning of suicide may not apply to all those choices that are literally acts of self-killing.

My reflections on suicide as a metaphor both for Jesus' notion of "the world" and for the milieu of our times are not meant to imply either that religious moralism which sees suicide simply as *sin,* or the moralism of psychology which looks at it in terms of *pathology.* Suicide, considered directly, opens us to the very mystery of existence. It is a revelation of the quality of human freedom and the transcendence to which it points.

Suicide implies the struggle that all of us deal with—parents, old friends, monks, college kids. The suicides are not a select group of separate characters. A thousand people are "officially" dead of suicide every day, but they are not the only ones who are faced with the constant choice between life and death. We all are. "No one ever lacks a good reason for suicide," wrote Cesare Pavese shortly before he killed himself. Albert Camus, who died alone in a car smashed against a tree, began *The Myth of Sisyphus* by stating, "There is only one question worth discussing, the question of suicide."

What is the reality of *sin* if not, in Daniel Stern's phrase, the habit of "using aspects of suicide" against ourselves? We might lack the nerve to commit the final act, and we may not recognize our "sinful" tendencies for what they are, but day in and day out we confront the problem of our innate attraction to self-destruction. We live in a world that encourages the small daily acts of negation that prepare us for the great one. There are meanings of suicide that neither the courts nor the dic-

tionaries admit, but that make it impossible for us to
regard those thousand people a day who do themselves
in as very different from us. They are not necessarily
"sick" or "sinners," but simply our sisters and brothers.
And who are we? We are the resigned housewives, the
compulsive playboys, the despairing priests, the addicted
teenagers, the reckless drivers, the bored bureaucrats, the
lonely salesmen, the smiling stewardesses, the restless
drifters, the walking wounded—"all of mankind engaged
in the massive conspiracy against their own lives that is
their daily activity." (Daniel Stern, in Alvarez, *The Savage
God,* p. 75). It may be nothing more than the steadfast
commitment to sameness. The simplest form of suicide
is the act of refusing the adventures and challenges and
changes that offer themselves to us everyday. "No thanks,"
we say. "I prefer not to," we murmer, like Melville's
Bartleby, preferring to stare at the wall outside the window. Preferring, as I do on especially bad days, to stay
in bed.

Such is the life that we build in our culture now that
we find it difficult, some nights, to remember what happened to the day. The drab uniformity that has come
to characterize much of contemporary life is an aspect
of suicide that we use against ourselves. The vaunted
materialism of the so-called free world implies, ironically
enough, a suicide of the senses. Commerce is built largely
on the selling of nonbeing. We spend billions on highways
and chain restaurants and stores that are all designed to
look, taste, smell, and feel exactly like each other. When
we pay to go some place, from New York to Sioux City
or Dallas, what we buy, in effect, is nontravel. When we
stay at home, we are nonentertained. Even such common

experiences as eating and conversation are devalued by the seemingly infinite hunger for instant hamburgers and televised football. The coincidence of economy, media, and government deprives us of that varied culture ordinary people instinctively build, with its peculiar sights, smells, traditions, tales, and customs. The suicide of an entire population is implicit in the idea that "what's good for General Motors is good for the country."

Suicide, therefore, is not simply an individualist phenomenon, a private final solution. Whole cultures struggle with it. The instinct for self-destruction that we all deal with is part of the moral impoverishment of societies in which people are bored and have become accustomed to uniformity. The other side of blandness is violence. Society's self-destructive urge increasingly takes the form of armed assault against those who are different, even to the point of genocide.

Seventy years of nearly continuous warfare in which a hundred million people have died, of calculated indifference to the unnecessary deaths of millions of others, the most recent example of which is the worldwide drought and famine between the tenth and thirteenth parallels, make our century one in which self-destruction has been at the center of human effort. We have abetted the suicide of chronic drug addiction not only by ignoring its roots in social inequity, but by tolerating the corruptions of government that make it possible. We have sponsored the absurd suicide of the American Dream in Vietnam. The Catholic Church, in good Roman fashion, has fallen on its own sword of rigid structures and doctrines at a time of massive cultural mutation. And at the root of it all, every fear takes its dread meaning from the new alpha-omega, the prospect of worldwide suicide by nuclear warfare.

Against such a background of potential and realized catastrophe, the difference between such daily problems as a broken-down car and the cosmic tragedy of nuclear war becomes blurred. In a world in which horror is commonplace, one grows used to it. The hallmark of suicide is indifference. Indifference to one's own fate or the fate of one's fellows. The ultimate humiliation of those imprisoned under the Nazi regime was to discover the ease with which one can become accustomed to horror, the ease with which one can take despair for granted. "It is a small matter," one hears oneself saying. "It is nothing to me."

"Humanity that has lost all meaning or believes it has can only wish to disappear or, at best, remain indifferent to the likelihood of its disappearance," wrote Emmanual Mounier. In our time such indifference amounts to the equivalent of the "throwing oneself down" that the Evil One invites. There is a nihilism in the air that affects our deepest selves and takes shape in the institutions of our culture. *Nihil.* Nothing. The world invites each of us to say, "I am nothing," and thereby to accustom ourselves to horror; to say, "I am not," and so to remain indifferent to history. In the case of dispossessed peoples, the world literally invites men and women to say, "I do not exist."

Obviously the milieu of suicide extends not only to private existential anxieties, but also to political and economic structures and systems. In the United States we had been accustomed to thinking of stereotypical regimes that force from their people the response of mind that says "I am nothing; the state is all." Now that the blinders have been removed, we discover the totalitarian character of our own age and place in the fact that morality, "democratic" policy, and the media all seem to disregard the choices and questions and intuitions of the single person. The mass-age totalitarianism we are faced with may or may not exist as an organized political phenomenon, but clearly there is a cultural state of mind in which initiative, creativity, and moral responsibility are stifled, while indifference is considered the height of sophistication.

The Vietnam war exemplified perfectly the state of mind of mass nihilism. Suddenly the "good citizen" of the United States of America was the one who said "I am nothing," the one who, in his consideration of the morality and politics of national policy, remained indifferent. Silent. Trusting someone else to make choices, to bear responsibility. It was the suicide of conscience. People who argue that Americans or their leaders are evil because of what they did in Vietnam do not understand that the milieu of suicide is deadly precisely because *good* men and women could pursue so rationally such an evil end. And no one of those who created the American war in Vietnam has admitted responsibility for it. The war criminals did not exist, and that was their crime.

The war was started by someone else, fought by someone else, continued by someone else; the bombs dropped by someone else. The reply to every question was "Not me." Except the question about death. The only ones who weren't "someone else" were the ones who got killed. And who was responsible? The courts said, "I'm not." The congress said, "I'm not." The pilots said, "I'm not." Billy Calley said, "I'm not." Westmoreland said, "I'm not." The taxpayers said, "I'm not." The bishops said, "I'm not." The president said, "I'm not." The machinery of American warfare gave us all something to deny.

The "machinery of war" includes more than what the fashionably "radical"—among whom I squirm to be counted—are prone to point out. In addition to the weapons, systems of exploitation, and totalitarian tendencies in political structures, there is the entire ambiance of nihilism that mistakes cynical wit for humor, the lack of commitment for freedom, the death of fetuses for the liberation of women, and the repudiation of transcendence for mental maturity. The patterns of moral suicide that Vietnam manifested infect all of us, in every aspect of our social lives. The "Evil One," as Jesus calls him, has his power and it is considerable. It is power over each of us. The thing about evil is that it is evil. It is dangerous. It is deadly. "There are no words in any human language," wrote a Hiroshima survivor, "which can comfort guinea pigs who do not know the cause of their death" (Alvarez, *The Savage God*, p. 236).

It is up to us to refuse the role of guinea pig. We are human beings who have been given the choice between life and death. We seek a language with which to speak, even after Hiroshima. Before the next exercise of moral horror. If we step to the edge of the abyss, it is to defeat it. If we seek out the "Evil One," it is to spit in his eye. If we talk of suicide, it is to find another way to live. We are trying to speak about the unspeakable. We cannot be indifferent to our fates or to those of others. We are human beings in the world, not quite of it, trying privately, publicly, to "show an affirming flame" (Auden). To find "the axe for the frozen sea within us" (Kafka).

To mobilize the abundant resources of life against the nothing heart of suicide.

I have never tried to kill myself. I do not take sleeping pills or drive at breakneck speeds. I do not think of myself as a doomed figure. But in the notion of suicide there is a metaphor that describes *my* condition as well as "the world's." I recognize in myself the romantic attraction to failed promise, the adolescent attitude toward death as a solution to problems, a vengeance against the indifference of others.

I have discovered the tendency toward self-destruction in the most ordinary aspects of my life. One summer in Michigan I took a canoe trip with three friends. We drove for hours to the northern woods, determined not to let the endless June rains stop us. Finally we got to the river. It should have been a tame enough trip. The river was popular with amateurs. No big adventure, no high danger.

But by the time we arrived the rains had swollen the river, made it muddy and very fast. The four of us stood on the bank watching it race by us. None of us spoke until I said, "Wow, it's really moving." And then we all laughed because we were all afraid. Instead of going on the river that day we played bridge for hours in a soaking tent.

The next day the rain stopped. In spite of the fact that the river was still fast, still high, we agreed, out of boredom or residual machismo, that we would go. Just as we were about to put in our canoes a local man happened by. "There's folks lived here all their lives," he said with alarm, "who wouldn't go on that river today." As he stood there waiting for a reply we looked at each other. It was a long way to come to play bridge. We could see fear in each other's eyes. We debated it again, but only for a moment. "Hell, let's do it!" one of us said. And we did.

But not for long. The current brought us quickly to a rapids that could have caused problems even without the swells of the rain. That day it nearly killed us. The lead boat turned over in the swift current, and one of my friends nearly drowned. The boat I was in did not tip; my companion and I were lucky enough to get to the river bank before we hit the most dangerous water. During the few seconds between passing my nearly drowned friend from the lead boat, desperately struggling to stay alive, and hitting the solid earth of the shore, I had a feeling in my stomach that told me I was going to die. I did not, of course, but in a flash came the inevitable question: Why was I doing this? Was there something more than mere foolishness that drove us to dare such danger? Is "mere foolishness" a cousin to chosen self-destruction? Is the irrational pursuit of "manhood" and the continual need to assert one's "bravery" in the face of risk a contemporary American version of the ancient act of suicide? When one exposes oneself to such a deadly and even likely possibility of disaster, is one in the grip of the old chaos again? Such questions are not easily answered, but neither can they be ignored.

The fact of death and the discovery of the power it has, not only over the brightest of poets and artists or the structures of society, but over oneself as well, leads to a better understanding of the need we have of a language of transcendence. Going down into the abyss and finding *nothing itself* leads to a new sense of the importance of belief. Perhaps the crisis of our age can be represented by the metaphor of self-destruction because in our age the language that offers access to transcendence is lacking. And so suicide, which denies the possibility of transcendent and graced intervention, becomes a common option. Deprived of words with which to speak to death, one submits to it.

In this pilgrimage of mine I have been seeking what is beyond myself and my people precisely *in* myself and my people. Out of what is basic to our existence we seek to affirm what is transcendent. If we are, in the end, religious, it is only because religious belief implies the refusal to become accustomed to horror and despair. "Of the world as it exists," Theodore Adorno said, "one cannot be enough afraid" (Alvarez, *The Savage God,* p. 113). But belief insists that "the world as it exists" has its being in what is beyond it, has its being in a life that is the opposite of suicide.

Our loss of the old identities, words, and structures of affirmation makes us more vulnerable than ever to the "Evil One," whose chief assault consists in the denial of the transcendent life that is beyond the world as it exists. Through turbulence and brutal loneliness and the mockery of the institutionalized word that will not risk the silence, one goes on seeking grace and reverence. It is a search, finally, for the changed name of God, the name we might learn again when the "Evil One" asks us whose we are.

The name of God is changing in our time.
What is his winter name?
Where was his winter home?

Ekëlof said there is a freshness
nothing can destroy in us—
not even we ourselves.
Perhaps that
Freshness is the changed name of God.

John Logan, "Spring of the Thief"

6

The Name of God

I have made your name known to the men you took from the world to give me. . . . Keep those you have given me true to your name so that they may be one like us. While I was with them I kept those you had given me true to your name. I have watched over them and not one is lost except the one who chose to be lost. (John 17:6, 11-12)

In their struggle against "the world" Jesus does not leave his friends helpless. He has revealed to them the key to his own victory over the "Evil One." Not surprisingly, it has to do with his relationship with *Abba.* Indeed, the "name" of *Abba* is what enables them to overcome the impulse to throw themselves down. In an explicit reference to suicide, Jesus contrasts the self-destructive betrayal of Judas with being "true to the name" of *Abba.*

The name of God is what will keep his friends safe in their conflict with "the world." In fact, the protective power of the name of God was already an old theme among

97

the people of Israel: "The name of the Lord is a strong
tower. The just one runs to it and is safe" (Prov. 18:10).

How do we get beyond the dull shield of learned indifference that keeps religious language and the words of
Jesus in particular from meaning anything to us? What
is this "name of God"? How can it protect against "the
world," the "Evil One," especially if those terms have
moved from their usual place on the pillows of rhetoric
and refer to the dread temptation and reality of suicide?

According to Raymond Brown, in John's Gospel the
phrase "name of God" always refers to the name the Lord
gave himself when Moses asked him who was speaking
(Commentary, *The Anchor Bible*, 29:751).

*Then Moses said to God, "I am to go, then, to the sons
of Israel and say to them. 'The God of your fathers has
sent me to you.' But if they ask me what his name is, what
am I to tell them?" And God said to Moses, "I AM WHO
I AM: This is what you must say to the sons of Israel;
'I AM has sent me to you. . . .' This is my name for all
time; by this name I shall be invoked for all generations
to come." (Exod. 3:13-15)*

God speaks the name the people need most to hear.
The people were slaves in Egypt. They were indifferent
to their fate because any other state of mind was so dangerous. They were accustomed to the horrors of slavery. At
the Pharaoh's inducement they had the habit of saying,
"I am nothing. I am not."

To *these* people God sends the messenger with the
revelation of his name. And his name itself is the proclamation of liberation: "I AM sent me!" Moses declares. "Get

up! Stand! Seize your freedom! Your slavery has come to
an end!" Since they are the people of God, they have the
right to speak his name as their own. I AM: it is the
opposite of suicide. I AM: it is the end of passive submission to oppressive power. I AM: it is the refusal of humiliation.

But how is the God of our fathers and mothers our God?
How do the experience of our people and the claims of
our age combine to prepare us to meet God now? The
response of God, according to the memory of Israel, is
the only response that could make sense from one generation to another. God's name is I AM. To be alive is to
speak God's name as if it were your own.

In an age when we are invited by so much that we
experience to say "I AM NOT," the response we most
require from God is his name for all time: I AM. The
slavery which humiliates us, turning us into nobodies,
is more subtle than Pharaoh's, but nearly as dangerous.
It is the slavery of the all too easy embrace of death. "In
every age," Robert Lifton has written, "man faces a persua-
sive theme which defies his engagement and yet must be
engaged. In Freud's day it was sexuality and moralism.
Now it is unlimited technological violence and absurd
death" (Alvarez, *The Savage God,* p. 269). The work of
Evil in our age, as in the Egypt-age of Israel, is the prom-
ulgation of I AM NOT. It occurs in the small traumas
of personal alienation. And it occurs on the massive
scale of genocide. The act of engagement is I AM. God's
name is the ultimate act of resistance against the milieu
of suicide. The I AM becomes more critical than ever
as we understand the meaning in a nuclear age of the
possibility of a total, final I AM NOT.

The I AM of God is a name with which every human being, however tempted to nihilism, has some capacity to identify. When we recognize the I AM in our midst, whether from ourselves or another, there immediately emerge possibilities for freedom and meaning that we did not see when overwhelmed with the I AM NOT. Every enslaved community and every oppressed people has its tales about men and women who defied horror and spoke the affirming word, thereby enabling others to do so.

I think of the story about a young singer who was among the thousands imprisoned in the National Stadium in Chile after the coup that overthrew Salvador Allende. His I AM began with a solitary song that he sang as he stood among the frightened and demoralized prisoners. Someone passed him a guitar and soon hundreds, then thousands, of people were singing with him. His spirit was contagious. The people joined him in proclaiming I AM. In effect, they sang WE ARE.

The authorities were threatened by the power tangibly moving through the crowd of prisoners. Whether by policy or panic, some of the guards seized the young singer and took him away. When he returned to the other prisoners, not only had his guitar been smashed, but his fingers had been cut off. As he walked into the midst of the people, they withdrew from him, silent, horrified. He walked out to the middle of an open space, lifted his bloody, fingerless hands, and began to sing as before. It was the I AM all over again. The people sang with him. Predictably, the guards returned, seized him, and took him away.

When the singer walked into their midst the next time, blood trickled from his mouth. His tongue had been cut out. As he stood again in the open space, some wept, but most of those who saw him remained silent. Then, after standing motionless for a time, the young man began swaying to and fro. Some thought he was about to faint, but his movement had a grace and deliberation about it. Finally they saw that it was a dance. I AM, he danced. Soon hundreds of people were moving in the silent, graceful sway of the young man's act of life in the face of death. And soon the guards came back and, in front of the people, shot him dead. But they did not kill his spirit.

In his novel *Breakfast of Champions* (Delacorte Press/ Seymour Lawrence, 1973), Kurt Vonnegut reports on the healing power of the I AM even when it comes from as weak and halting a man as Rabo Karabekian. He is an artist who donates one of his abstract paintings to the people of Midland City. When he overhears citizens in a bar deriding his work, Karabekian's response surprises even his own creator. Vonnegut injects his own reaction as author into the story: "I did not expect Rabo Karabekian to rescue me. I had created him, and he was in my opinion a vain and weak and trashy man, no artist at all. But it is Rabo Karabekian who made me the serene Earthling which I am this day" (p. 220).

Vonnegut describes how Karabekian, listening to the ridicule of the people in the bar, gradually found it in himself to reply; he "slid off his barstool so he could face all those enemies standing up" (p. 220). "The painting did not exist," he says, "until I made it. Now that it does exist, nothing would make me happier than to have it reproduced again and again, and vastly improved upon by all the five-year-olds in town. I would love for your children to find pleasantly and playfully what it took me many angry years to find.

"I now give you my word of honor," Karabekian continues, "that the picture your city owns shows everything about life which truly matters. . . . It is a picture of the awareness of every animal. It is . . . the 'I AM' to which all messages are sent. It is all that is alive in any of us" (p. 221).

The act of I AM is standing up. It is the opposite of throwing yourself down, as the "Evil One" suggests. It is the opposite of lying down in humiliation, of staying in bed all day, of crawling, of walking on one's knees. In showing his mastery over death, Jesus says to Lazarus in the tomb, "Get up and come out" (John 11:43). He says to the paralyzed man at the pool, "Stand up and walk" (John 5:8). When the sea threatens, he stands on its surface (John 6:16). When his friends throw themselves to the ground in fear, he says, "Stand up. Don't be afraid" (Matt. 17:8).

When Jesus prays, *"Abba,* glorify your son so that your son may glorify you" (John 17:1-5), he is saying the time has come for him to *stand up.* Glory is "a visible manifestation of majesty through an act of power" (Raymond Brown, *Anchor Bible,* 29:753). When everything in his time and place invites a man to lie down, passive, ignored, imprisoned, and when in the face of *that* experience he stands up, *that* is an act of power. It is the act of power that points to transcendence. In the presence of courage where fear alone is allowed one can only say, "There is more here than meets the eye." When a woman stands up in the face of what pushes her down, the fact that she is in a communion of power with some source of life beyond her becomes visible to everybody.

It was that way with Michele Murray, the critic and poet who died of cancer recently. I counted myself among her followers, read her reviews, relished her poems. She refused the reductions to sex roles and utilitarian functions the world tries to force on women. Her writings revealed a spirit of toughness and self-affirmation that allowed her to stand against, at the difficult end, death itself. In *A House of Good Proportion: Images of Women In Literature* (Simon and Schuster, 1973), she wrote, not only for feminists but for all of us: "The imagination brings to fruition infinite possibilities, it annihilates nothing, it charges all our being with meaning too rich to be fully conveyed, yet sustaining us in the operations of our life."

Michele Murray died at home in the midst of her family and her books, not protected from death's coming by ignorance or the oblivion of drugs. Colman McCarthy wrote in the *Washington Post,* "The last hours of her life were a stirring resistance against the tyranny of death." On a couch in her library Ms. Murray talked individually with three of her four children—David, 18; Jonathan, 16; and Sarah, 13. According to McCarthy, she told them she would die soon, though she didn't know when, and that she had enjoyed being their mother. And offered them some thoughts she had on how they might live after her death. The next day her husband, Jim, read her the joyful Psalms, kissed her, prayed with her, and she died. The courage with which she embraced her life even in the face of its conclusion is revealed in her "Death Poem":

What will you have when you finally have me?
Nothing.
Nothing I have not already given

freely each day I spent
not waiting for you
but living
as if the shifting shadows of grapes
and fine-pointed leaves in the shelter
of the arbor would continue to tremble
when my eyes were absent
in memory of my seeing,
or the books fall open where I marked them
when my astonishment overflowed
at a gift come unsummoned, this love
for the open hands of poems,
earth fruit, sun soured grass, the steady
outward lapping stillness of midnight
snowfalls, an arrow of light waking me
on certain mornings with sharp wound
so secret that not even you
will have it when you have me.
You will have my fingers
but not what they touched. Some gestures
outflowing from a rooted being, the memory
of morning light cast on a bed
where two lay together—
the shining curve of flesh!—
they will forever be out of your reach
whose care is with the husks.

When "a Word becomes flesh," as John says, "we behold glory" (1:14). That is the moment when a person stands up and bears witness to the truth. The old proverb takes on new meaning; one word of truth outweighs the world. Outweighs even death. It is what the people saw in Chile that day. And it is what Michele Murray's readers had dimly sensed throughout her life and what her family saw in radiance at the end. And it is what Pilate saw one day in his court in Judea.

The story of Jesus' I AM begins with his own proclaimed sense of oneness with God, revealed in his use of the intimate form of address, *Abba*. Because God is himself the ultimate act of I AM, Jesus, as son, is the act of I AM in the flesh.

Jesus' intimacy-to-life with one he calls *Abba* reverses the intimacy-to-death that so often allows resentment and misunderstanding to overcome love. Our I AM NOT is contagious. We pass it on as if it were a disease. Indeed, we inherit the habit of self-killing in all its disguises. We are, as we used to say, born with original sin. It is not a matter of focusing on the sins of the parents as if they were the unique source of the child's disorientation. The self-doubt and tendency to self-destruction of the parent is part of the world's self-doubt. Nevertheless, the child encounters it first and above all in the parent.

Vonnegut states that his own character's I AM in *Breakfast of Champions* went far in healing the I AM NOT he inherited as a boy. Commenting on his own experience as author of the story, he writes: " 'This is a very bad book you're writing,' I said to myself. 'I know,' I said. 'You're afraid you'll kill yourself the way your mother did,' I said. 'I know,' I said" (p. 193).

The poet Sylvia Plath understood her own struggle with suicide as one she inherited from her father, who had died suddenly when she was a girl, leaving her desolate. The poem that describes her first attempt at suicide is entitled "Daddy," which is, of course, our commonest word for *Abba.* "At twenty I tried to die," she tells her dead father, "and get back, back, back to you." The words reflect Plath's longing for the communion that she had known with her father and that had been ruptured by his death. Ultimately, she was dealing not simply with the loss of a cherished parent but with the loss of an ability to trust one's communion with life itself.

This urge to return to the primordial intimacy with one's loved parent is reflected in the words of Jesus: "I am not in the world any longer, *Abba.* I am coming to you" (John 17:1). Sylvia Plath's suicide is a consequence of her own inability to reclaim the communion with life that she associates with her father. And so she writes, "Daddy, Daddy, you bastard, I'm through." Jesus goes down the same dark well, but finds something different: "I finished the work you gave me to do. Now, *Abba,* it is time for you to glorify me" (17:4).

The importance of Jesus to us is that he discovered at the center of his life the "I AM to which all messages are sent." In Jesus the I AM NOT is overcome, or, as he says himself, "I have overcome the world" (16:33). This is at least partly a matter of his relationship with God the *Abba,* the one from whom he has a clear, unambiguous sense of communion with all that exists. The death-trend of generations gives way to the life-trend in Jesus. Though he freely submits to the effects of the I AM NOT milieu, the effects of his graced inheritance make Jesus unique. The first hint of his glory is his immense sense of himself. He is who he is. A sign of this is the ease with which he uses the first person pronoun, employing the words "I" or "me" sixty times in the course of the prayer (John 17) that has been the basis for this reflection. He does not, in other words, suffer from the underdeveloped ego that leads to the sham masculinity that constantly needs to exhibit its power. At the same time, he does not suffer from egoism; his uses of "I" refer always to the *Abba,* from whom he exists, or to his friends, for whom he exists. Whenever the I AM is uttered in integrity, not only does the person stand for himself or herself, but also and simultaneously for all others. The act of I AM, reflecting and sharing in God's life-giving act of I AM, has nothing in common with the narrow self-preoccupation that characterizes individualist philosophies.

So, when Jesus invokes the name of God, "the strong tower," he invokes the life-source itself as a protection for his friends. "It is I," he says to them on the storming sea, "Do not be afraid" (6:28). The first example of how the name protects them comes in the very next chapter of John, as Jesus' confrontation with the "Evil One" begins when soldiers come to arrest him.

"Who are you looking for?" he asks. They answer, "Jesus the Nazarene." When Jesus replies, "I AM HE," "they moved back and fell to the ground" (18:5-8). Jesus then sets the terms for his own arrest, demanding that they leave his friends free and unharmed. He allows himself to be taken away, but he does so with immense dignity, freedom, and an utter lack of humiliation. In the face of their shallow threat, he asserts himself in the name of the *Abba:* I AM.

His Father's name is the "truth" to which he "came to bear witness" (17:17), not so much in what he said but in how he lived. The climax of Jesus' struggle with "the world" comes when the question is squarely put to

him, the question with infinite implications. His whole
life had been practice for this moment. It harkens back
to Moses asking God his name, and forward to guards
interrogating a singer in the stadium prison of Chile.

"Are you a king then?" Pilate asks.

"It is you who say it," Jesus replies. "I AM. I was born
for this. I came into the world for this: to bear witness
to the truth, and all who are on the side of truth listen
to my voice."

"Truth?" Pilate repeats. "What is that?" And with
that he goes out to the people and says, "I find no case
against this man."

It is a moment in which we can all see ourselves. We
too wash our hands of responsibility, equivocate, and
answer, in one way or another, "I AM NOT." I am not
responsible. I am not in charge. I am not smart enough.
I am not, am not, am not. We can be Peter: "I am not
his friend." We can be Judas: "The one I kiss, him. Not
me."

What we need to learn is what Pilate was too "prudent"
to assert: that the I AM outweighs every I AM NOT. We
can choose to be "true to the name" (17:12). This affirmation of one's own selfhood is not a sales technique, nor
self-hypnosis; it has nothing to do with the superficial
acts of self-confidence recommended by "positive thinking." The truth to which Jesus points with his life and
death is that each person is burdened/gifted with a divine
act of existence.

I remember one of the moments in my youth when
I understood the implications of my own existence. Like
most children I grew up thinking that human life was
largely a matter of doing what someone else wanted you

to do. Before coming of age, aren't we all busy meeting each other's expectations, playing out socially approved roles in return for status and meaning? When the church is experienced immaturely, for example, isn't it the community in which sons and daughters worship because their parents tell them to, or in which parents worship only to set a good example for their kids, or in which parents and children together worship rather than disappoint Sister, who's given up so much, or Father, who tries so hard? The community of the immature is the place where no one does anything for himself or herself. It's all for someone else's benefit.

I admitted one day that such a web of altruism would not hold me for long. If I was going to be in the church or part of any other common effort, it would have to be for my own sake as well as for that of others. The awareness that selfhood is not the same thing as selfishness came to me when I was sitting in the outcrop of an old tree's roots overhanging Lake George. I was paging through Edward Steichen's *Family of Man,* which had fallen open on a full-page photograph of a screaming newborn child. The words printed as a caption shot through me like lightning: "The entire universe resounds with the cry 'I AM.'" I remember standing up in the roots of that tree and throwing my arms over my head and letting out the yell that was my long-forgotten birthscream. I was twenty-three years old, but it was the first day of my manhood. It was the first time I'd said I AM with any sense of the magnificent creation those words made me.

I had discovered in myself what is beyond myself, the Self in my self. I had touched the "freshness nothing can destroy in us not even we ourselves" (John Logan). Sud-

denly there was a sense of the meaning of belief, of communion with all that is, and I understood that freshness
is "the changed name of God." It was the "dearest freshness
deep down things" (Gerard Manley Hopkins). It was the
moment when I claimed ownership of the core of being
that is the source of imagination, hopes, and courage—
in Coleridge's great phrase, "the repetition in man of the
creative I AM of God."

God's name is revealed in the experience each of us
has of living consciously in the face of death. Jesus' use
of the *Abba* metaphor suggests that God is intimately a
matter of the gift of life and nurture that we commonly
experience first and perhaps most fully in the embrace
of a parent. The sense of "primary relatedness" transcends
the sense of "primary ambivalence" (Erik Erikson). The
name of God vanquishes the equivocation that paralyzes,
enabling us to call upon the freshness in ourselves as the
dominant feature of our lives.

Kirilov, in Dostoevsky's *The Possessed,* puts it negatively
when he says, "All man did was to invent God, so as to
live without killing himself." One needn't agree with the
character to appreciate the insight. The sustained decision
to live, while walking day after day through an atmosphere
deadly with the lure of suicide, is very much bound up
with a felt sense of transcendence in one's life, whatever
the means or level of its articulation. The I AM of each
person is his or her primary source of the revelation of
God's I AM.

From the beginning of all time, the Word was the cry
I AM of God. God *resounds* with this Word. At the time
of the Annunciation, when the Word became flesh, it
joined us in the slow process of self-realization, of getting

up the nerve and learning how to yell. The Word in its cry continually invades all the words we abandon as lies and so makes truth not only possible for us, but very nearly habitual.

"Truth? What is truth?" Poor Pilate, he deserves more sympathy than we commonly offer. By the time Pilate encounters his strange prisoner, Jesus has already claimed ownership of his own I AM, has fully known that he is himself the Truth. There is an opening on transcendence in the embrace of one's own existence. This proclamation of Jesus is also, Paul says, the demand of discipleship: "Now before God the source of all life and before Jesus Christ who made his good profession of the Truth in front of Pontius Pilate, I put to you the duty of being who you say you are" (1 Tim. 6:13).

If we can claim to cry I AM, to be who we say we are, it is because we too discover in ourselves a heart we hadn't known we had. We *claim* it. We *stand* with it. Its only hoard is freshness. Its habit, though we are awkward with it and embarrassed to talk of it, is the knowledge of God.

I have made your name known to the ones you took from the world to give me. They were yours and you gave them to me. . . . They know you the only true God. (John 17:3-6)

We know more than we think. We are more alive than we suppose. We live now with life to the full, what John calls "eternal life." And we *know* it in those moments when *we* resound with the cry of the universe that is in us and beyond us. The echoes come like the shudders of lovers whose "knowing" is intimate and of the flesh, always ready for silence and the Word, for either or both. Hearts full of nothing, hearts broken, hearts of "the world." But hearts together in freshness and its promise: "I will give them a new heart to know me. And they shall be my people and I will be their God" (Jer. 24:7).

Family of God

I survive the conspiracy against self
that my own life mounts.
I am fresh, always starting again,
ready to go,
saying to defeat's eye
beat it you bastard.

I choose to live when I can
think of reasons not to.
That's freedom.
All the power I want.

My bad days are bad. It shows.
I have heard people pray for me.
I read myself in Pavese, Plath, John Berryman.
I write about death as if it were
my backyard. In fact my backyard
is the oldest graveyard in Boston.

Some nights I think I am going to die
but don't.
Because I'd want to write about it afterwards
and send it on to Harper's.
Some rejection slips are deadly
as a Black September valentine to Golda Meir.
So it seems to me on my bad days
which are bad.

But they have their little secret,
their trick, their *mystery,* if you want.
It is mine.
I have this need of an evening
to look for midnight
and at midnight to look for dawn.
Neither satisfies but both suffice.
Curiosity hampers selfishness, thank God.
The future keeps the past
from being bored with now.

My darkness and my light
are nipples to each other, nurturing.
Such milk, such graciousness
is smiling absolution
for all my aging infancy.

I am thinking, forgive me, of my Mom.
Life is a mother like my own to me.
She is good.
Real good. She taught me
what I still learn; how not to starve
or die from want of being held.

If she was here now
I would hug her hard.
Instead I choose again to live

Remembering my mother's embrace, seeing her now, rocking in the old chair and holding her grandchild to her breast, I realize why Jesus chooses the word *Abba* to describe the experience he has of communion with all that exists. He applies the word to God. But incarnation means he learned what he knew of God, even what of God he was in himself, from and with and through the men and women who shared his time and place. I see him in the cradle of a woman's arms, as an infant and as a dead man, and I understand the motherhood-fatherhood that gave him life, even through death.

I am thinking again of my mother. Of the embrace that taught me heaven. Of the farewell that sent me off to manhood. I am thinking of her temper, her pushing, her anger, her pique. Of the silence she could inflict on us in her moods. But through it all there was the consistent act of love, teaching us in the morning that the day and its dangers were not too much for us. I know now that when the I AM NOT offers itself as an alternative, I can respond with the I AM I inherit from Mary Anne Morrissey Carroll.

During the time my father was the Director of the Defense Intelligence Agency, a red hot-line phone waited to ring in my parents' bedroom with an announcement of World War III. It was part of the emergency phone network that linked the White House with the military leadership, with the people who would give the last desperate orders of war. There were only two reasons that

phone would ring: one would be the imminent possibility
of war; the other, the occasional test of the system. Several
times the red phone rang while we were at dinner. When
that happened a dread stillness would settle over the table
while my father left the room to answer. Always prepared
for the worst, I *expected* disaster. I *expected* my dad to
rush from the house, kissing us all briefly. But what I
remember most about that awful stillness in which I
tormented myself with fears was my mother's breaking
in by saying, "Eat your potatoes, Jim." "Elbow off the
table, Kevin." "Pass the butter, Joe." Saying, in effect,
"Look, the only thing to do at a moment like this is to
eat, live, be alive. Don't give in to horror." As it turned
out, the phone was only being tested when it rang in my
presence.

Once, when I was gone, it rang for real, and my father
was off to the Cuban missile crisis. Even then, even if the
war *had* come, I can imagine my mother saying, "Eat.
It is more important now than ever. Eat. Pass the food,
please. Tell us what happened at school." I imagine my
mother insisting on life even in the face of *that* death.
Ordinary, calm, kindly life. Stern with death. Life itself
is the last refuge from panic, the final defeat of horror.
"Eat. Even now. Especially now."

The exhilaration, joy, and peace that come with the
act of I AM do not come without their price. There are
consequences, some of them difficult. Some of them well
known, if not obvious. Some of them hidden.

One of the consequences of the discovery of the I AM
of God in the I AM of one's own life is the loss of the
clear sense of who God is, apart from one's own existence.

If, in fact, "freshness is the changed name of God," it is a name that remains vague, elusive, and secular. The name I AM refuses every attempt people make to hem it in with religious words and categories. I AM will not be institutionalized. It is passed on from generation to generation, but not by religious formulae or the practice of cultic rituals. These have their part, but finally the knowledge of God's name is passed on by the act of motherhood-fatherhood itself. By the act of family, of human fellowship. God is known in the knowledge of existence. To remember that one exists is to remember God.

One of the consequences of this discovery is that there is no God "out there" who has a knowledge and a will for us apart from the knowledge and will we discover in ourselves. To discover that *that* God is gone is to know the "loss of God" that we commonly mistake for lost faith.

The abandonment that Jesus experiences in his passion and death is an inevitable consequence of his own revolutionary discovery of God's presence *in* his own act of existence. Because Jesus *dared* to name God, *dared* to call him *Abba,* to claim the intimacy of a common life-source with him, he *had* to experience "God" as absent at the very moment he asked to be rescued from suffering and death.

Jesus prayed, "Not my will but your will be done." But his prayer was met with silence. Jesus prayed, "If it is your will, remove this cup." But God did not speak to him. *Abba* did not hold him, hug him, save him from the fate he freely chose himself. Jesus had to face the consequences of his own proclamation, and the chief consequence was the fact that he was alone. Abandoned. Jesus had drawn his address for God from the analogy of family life. By that analogy the moment of his suffering was his rite of passage from youth to maturity, from the security of home to the risky freedom of independence. It was a passing-over which, in its pain and loneliness for both parent and child, is well known to all of us.

Jesus had said that God is present to him and to us in the way a loving parent is. We carry God in our hearts the way we carry all that gives us existence, the massive gift of the past and its issue in the flesh of the single man and woman whose act of love was our beginning. Once the rupture of independence occurs and we pass from childhood to adulthood, we are able to understand that we carry *that* gift of life in us as a continuing source of I AM, and not simply as a memory that is done with and over. That is why the killing of the past, whether through the repudiation of history or the hatred of one's parents, is always an aspect of suicide.

God is the act of existence *from* whom we receive ours. But the free act of existence is *for* ourselves and *for* our children. The parent who insists on being the one *for* whom the child exists as well as *from* whom the child has its being does the child an immense disservice. The past, beginning with our parents, demands two things of us: that we carry it in our hearts, and that we leave it behind, moving continually into times and territories that have never been explored before. God, the *Abba* of Jesus, required him to make choices that had never been made before, not even by God. Jesus' obedience is to freedom. The communion of *Abba* and Son includes the rupture, the experience of abandonment, independence. Jesus does not fake it.

He bears the terrible weight of his own discovery that

he is "one with the Father" (John 17:21-23). According to Raymond Brown's comment on this passage (*Anchor Bible,* 29:769), "one" in the usage of John has two meanings. It has the common and obvious sense of togetherness, communion—"The Father and I are one." But there is another, terrible meaning of the word. It also means alone, solitary, abandoned, independent. It is *that* meaning that Jesus tries to avoid, as he asks his Father to intervene, to take the suffering away. But the Father could not if he wanted to. The Father and son are alone to each other.

In this sense the climax of Jesus' relationship with his Father is not simply an act of mindless obedience. It is struggle, even conflict. As Jean Leclerque said in a lecture, "Jesus is not the victim of an unresolved oedipal complex." He is not reduced to infantile submission before a tyrannical parent. Instead, Jesus' final struggle with the *Abba* in his own passion and death is a struggle for mature and full life. There is a development from the beginning of his passion and the docile "your will be done" to the discovery on the cross that there is no "will of God" apart from his own freely chosen destiny. That moment wrenches from Jesus his own resisting, anguished act of I AM *before* and *against* his Father, with whom at the last he was not in felt communion. His heart was so "full of nothing it wanted to implode" (Jim Harrison, "Letters to Yesenin, I," *American Poetry Review* 2, no. 3 [1973]: 44). "My God, My God, why have you abandoned me?" "Daddy, Daddy, you bastard, I'm through" (Plath).

It is the inevitable moment between parents and child. In our time the movement from childhood to maturity is deprived of many of the great rituals of passage, the

sacramental moments of "passing-over." In an age that
prizes uniformity and submerges interpersonal conflict,
the various crisis-points of growth are rarely acknowl-
edged. When they cannot separate ritually and symboli-
cally, children and parents find it difficult to move away
from each other without killing their relationship altogether. Nevertheless, through all the conflict and struggle, ordinary people constantly find in themselves the
strength to grow up, to accept freedom, and to bless their
children as they leave.

I think of the moment between me and my dad, the
moment of confronting differences and living with them.
It lasted several years. It came late, beginning about the
time I stood on the roots of that tree at Lake George,
crying with the whole universe, I AM. Easy enough to do
by yourself in a tree. But try it at the kitchen table with
a father who has a master's degree in theology, a degree
in law, *magna cum*, and two magnificent careers, who is
half an inch taller, shows no signs of going bald, and, in
his sixties, shoots golf in the seventies. Not to mention the
fact that he is the most honest person you've ever met.

It so happened there was this war. It so happened that
the son wondered about it. The father knew the answers,
his office being close to the room where they kept the
maps and secret plans. The son remembers in the early
sixties driving his dad home from the Pentagon, where
he'd worked late. They didn't talk much; the red phone
was on the dashboard between them. The father looked
out the window at the lights of Washington while the
son watched his reflection in the corner of the big wrap-
around windshield. "Son," the father said softly, "one of
these nights I might not come home." The son listened,

pushed the ocean back down the well of his throat, knowing, of course, what his dad meant. It was the time between the Berlin wall and the Cuban missiles. His dad would be needed in Thunder Mountain, West Virginia, or wherever they kept the Button in emergencies. "And if that happens," his father was saying, "I won't even be able to call. So it'll be up to you and Joe. Just get Mom and the boys and go." It was the only time he'd ever spoken that way. He never would again. His dad didn't say where to go or how to get there. Even then the son knew there would be no place. No gas to get there. No time. Certainly not from Washington, ground zero. But it didn't matter. His father wasn't talking about the escape of the family at all; he was simply weighed down by the dread fatalism common to war planners in an age of terror. The man was really just saying that he was the boy's father, and that the boy was the man's son. It was a union and a bond, fashioned mainly of silence and shared fear and love of the family and the strange intimacy of a nighttime drive that nothing could ever break. They would be father and son forever; not even World War III could separate them. But—who would have guessed?—a lousy little war in the swollen finger of Asia came out of nowhere and almost did.

I am among those whose I AM was not fully said until we had said it about Vietnam. I was late to it, and slow and timid to the end. Though I shared the exemption of clergy, even that was not protection against the choice. The "Hell, no, we won't go!" of the early refusers found its place eventually in my voice. In the end I found out who I was in the act of rejecting that war. In my case the choice was the product less of courage or integrity—my body

was never on the line—than of the new influences and
attitudes the age forced on me. But for all of us the decision *against* national policy was a wrenching lesson in
what it means to be an American. And for those of us
who loved the church, the church's alliance with the war
was a wrenching lesson in what it means to be a believer.
And for some fewer the decision *against* was a wrenching
lesson in what it means to be a son.

I thought that if I disagreed with my father it would kill
me. I had begun the decade imitating him, serving as an
ROTC cadet. I thought that if I disapproved of the project
to which he was giving the best years of his life it would
kill him. Eventually, though, I learned that my father's
act of existence, the sense of his own integrity, did not
depend on my agreement or approval. His I AM was not
waiting for mine, and that is what he taught me. Mine
could not wait for his. Although my disapproval grew to
horror, anger, and shame, my father survived and so did I.

The fact was, he loved me. I loved him. Our relationship
sustained the love even through several years when our
conversation was mainly about baseball. We never "talked
it out" or "worked it through." Neither did we slug each
other. But we knew. We were alone to each other, alone
as only a war can make people. Conscious of the real and
brutal burden that war was inflicting on soldiers and pea-
sants thousands of miles away, I knew that we were lucky,
war being what it is, that all we lost was a childhood sense
of each other's perfection.

Even before the United States' part in the war had
"ended"—though we are still underwriting the continuing
conflict with money and weapons—and even before my
father had retired from the service, we had come to a new

way of being father and son. In a way, having lost each
other, we found each other. It is not simply a matter of
occasional visits or long-distance conversations. More
and more importantly, it seems to me, it is this sense of
carrying that man in my flesh. The oneness of solitude
before him and independence from him is also the oneness of a physical intimacy that makes us both proud to
bear the same last name. My struggle to be not of him
was a sign of how very much of that man I am. Now when
I stand in the roots of a tree and cry I AM, I hear his voice
in my own.

Once the father has been accused, he can be trusted.
So Jesus goes from, "Why have you abandoned me?" to
"Into your hands I trust my spirit." The progression from
untested intimacy through rebellion and aloneness to
rediscovered trust is what John calls *glorification*. It is
also known as *resurrection*. The discovery that the initial
and primary relatedness to one's source and sustenance
withstands the plunge into alienation and aloneness, that
is the discovery around which Jesus gathers his followers.
It is what has made it possible, in our household, for
us to go on building a family during an insane time.

The sense of *Abba* which I discover in myself was
visibly manifested as the source of union for our family
through events that could otherwise have blown us finally
apart. One of my brothers, Dennis, was much more direct
and forthright than I in challenging the Vietnam war.
Because of age and circumstance he was subject to the
draft, and when the moment of choice arrived, he became
a resisting conscientious objector. It was his act of I AM,
and, naturally enough, there were intensely painful
moments around it. At first my dad was shocked and hurt.

My brother was living at home at the time, on an Air Force base, no less. There was an ongoing agony of silence and argument between them. There was an escalation that seemed to match every escalation of the war.

There was a family awareness that we all hovered over unmendable misunderstanding and resentment. Each of the five sons found himself in a different position on the issues and emotions that surfaced: one a psychologist, asking the right questions; one a priest, in the Berrigan wing; one an FBI agent, pursuing draft-resisters; one a conscientious objector; one a college student, preparing his own choices. And sustaining us through the conflict and confusion was the consistent love of my mother. It may be that she saw in each what was beyond all of us and therefore held us together. When Dennis repudiated a way of looking at the world and a system of values that she had long held in common with my dad, my mom responded with an absolutely faithful commitment to her son, all the while still supporting and nurturing her husband. Oh, there were some grand fights. Dennis's long hair drove her crazy. But finally she refused to let *that* become the issue. When Dennis became a vegetarian, she responded by preparing special meatless dishes for him while the rest of us ate the holiday turkeys. When Dennis showed up with his freaky friends, she stifled a lifetime of prizing a certain manner and appearance and offered them welcome to the table. She prepared the table around which the remarkable gathering broke bread: war objector, government agent, friend of fugitive, scientist, student, Air Force general, and the Irish woman whom they all loved and through whom they found ways to love each other.

Jesus uses the word *Abba,* as we have seen, to describe the discovery he made in his flesh that at the heart of everything there is a profound unity which nothing can finally disrupt. That sense of unity, we recall, is what Jesus described as the knowledge of God. It was eternal life, which in John's Gospel is not something waiting for us "in eternity" or "in the other world." It is life to the full, now. Eternal life is the consequence of a unique power, Jesus' power to sustain and manifest the unities of existence.

Through the power over all flesh that you have given your son, let him give eternal life to all those you have entrusted to him. And eternal life is this; to know you, the only true God and Jesus Christ whom you have sent.

To know in one's flesh and blood that the unity that one detects in family life is absolutely trustworthy is to know it in oneself. There had been hints in our house of the gift of life to the full, full enough to flourish despite intense and deeply felt differences. It is the knowledge of the name of God: I AM. And as each of us claims that name as his or her own, we discover the inevitable progress from I AM to WE ARE.

The power of the Son is not only power over "flesh," as Jesus says (John 17:2). It is also and especially power over the *Abba.* Such is the intimacy and bond between them that both are subject to the freedom of the other. It is in this sense that Israel believed that to *know* another was to assert power over that other. In particular, to know another's name was to have that other in some sense at your mercy. For this reason the name of God was not uttered by Jews, out of the sense that no creature has the right to claim such power, such knowledge of God.

The world has not known you, but I have known you. Jesus speaks the name of God, though it was forbidden to do so. "Before David was," he said, "I AM." Jesus asserts power over the *Abba* and, ludicrous as it may seem to say so, Jesus enables us to assert similar power over God. *I have made your name known to them and will continue to make it known.*

It is a further consequence of Jesus' discovery that God lives in him, and through him, in all human beings, the way a loving parent lives in a grown son or daughter. Grown children do not simply submit to their parents. The Son does not simply submit to the Father. In fact, just as the Father of Jesus, the life-source, is a principle of fresh-ness in his Son, so the Son, in his conflicting-affectionate relationship with the Father, is a source of freshness for Him also.

I know what I'm talking about. I have seen my own parents change, discover new meanings and struggle to be faithful to them, in their effort to survive the raising of five sons. The decade that began with my mother acting as a Pentagon hostess ended with her warmly receiving the radical friends of her son.

I happened to visit home once while Daniel Berrigan was still a fugitive, underground. A news report on television reminded us that he was successfully eluding the FBI. I made no comment, but wondered to myself if my brother Brian were on the case. Suddenly my mother said, "I wish he'd come here, that Father Berrigan." I looked at her, certain I knew her meaning. She revered the FBI and had a deep affection for J. Edgar Hoover that dated back to the forties, when my father worked for him. With an edge of cynicism in my voice I asked, "So you could turn him in?" "No," she replied, returning my hard look, "I would hide him." Then she smiled. "They'd never look for him here." I understood two things about my mother then, one old, one new. She still had an Irish loyalty to her priests. And by then she hated the war in Asia in the way that mothers have always learned to hate the wars that kill or nearly ruin their sons.

And my father was not immune to the challenge his children, especially Dennis, represented. In some ways my dad's act of I AM submitted to my brother's. Neither of them yielded to the other, but neither was unmoved. They stayed at each other for more than a year. My brother was having a hard time of it. When he applied for conscientious objector status, the board turned him down. He appealed and was turned down again. Finally there came the moment of his last appeal. If he were rejected again he'd have to decide whether to leave the country, join the underground, or go against his conscience and serve in the Army. It was a moment when the bond of our whole family was pushed nearly to the breaking point.

Dennis was informed that for the final appeal he could appear in the company of his lawyer. Well, my father is a lawyer. Dennis asked my father to go with him to his hearing, after several years of argument, hurt feelings, and mutual disapproval. My Dad went, general's uniform and all. He argued on his son's behalf, and the CO status was granted.

Later I was present when someone criticized Dennis in front of my father. My brother was not there, and I was on the other side of the room.

"General," the man said to my father, "I think it was big of you to support your son, but, frankly, I don't think your boy's attitude does him much credit."

"I suppose I should agree with you," my father replied, "I share your instincts. I've spent my whole life defending our point of view. But I don't think you understand my son's position well enough to see the point he has. I don't understand it either, though God knows I've tried to. All I know for sure is this: if human beings don't drastically change the way they resolve their conflicts with each other, we won't survive this century." And then, after a pause, my dad said, "My son Dennis certainly represents a drastic change from the way we were brought up. And that may be just the change we need."

Looking back, I can see that my brother is not so drastically different from my dad. They are both men of integrity. Even as they continue to reject each other's ideas, they are right to be, however awkwardly, proud of each other.

God is a "child-changed father" too, as Cordelia said of Lear. Though it violates the usual static, greeting-card version of religion, Jesus' assertion that God is *Abba* means that God is in a relationship of mutual influence and creativity with the Son. The Son and the *Abba* are clay in each other's hands. Or we might think of them as dancers, always moving, each responding to the partner's surprising rhythms. God is a companion in the Son's exploration of unmapped territory. They are both strangers to the future. So when the Son, unable in Gethsemane to turn his *Abba* into a pagan *deus ex machina* who would rescue him, discovers in the claims of his own experience the hard will of his life, the *Abba* recognizes that will as his own. The *Abba* discovers "God's will" in the Son.

It is a matter of our learning from our own upbringing, from our own parenthood, sonship, daughterhood. Life works, if we let it, to free us from a primitive Oedipal piety. We need not choose between a passive, rejected, and therefore approved Son and a crucifying but perversely forgiving Father. Instead we see them as we are to our parents—two acts of I AM in relation to each other. Where there is abandonment it is mutual, a consequence of two freedoms at work on each other. Where there is forgiveness and repossession, it goes both ways. As Jesus puts it in his prayer, "I have glorified you. It is time for you to glorify me" (John 17:4). Every parent must stand in awe and even worship before the mystery of a child who, as child, *creates*. Who does something wholly new. Who is alive in a unique way. To see oneself surpassed or completed or changed by one's offspring is to have the opening on transcendence that is proper to parenthood.

In addition to the parent-child analogy, John describes Jesus' relationship to God in terms of the analogy of the *Word*. The Father is changed by the Son in the way that the Author of Creation is changed by the Word he utters. A poet learns himself from the word he speaks. God learns who he is from the Word-made-flesh, watching, listening, confronting his own image in the flesh of the world and of Jesus. In speaking the word, William Chaplin says, the poet "destroys himself to make himself over through the reader" (*American Poetry Review* 2, no. 3 [1973]: 51). So do every father and mother destroy themselves against the child's freedom. The poet's relationship to his poem is not one of dominance, therefore, but of submission and creation. So of the parent to the child. The poem makes its own demands on the poet; it has its own existence, momentum, and meaning before which the poet bows with surprise and humility.

There is a generative, creative function for the reader of the poem. The self-destruction of the poet for the sake of his remaking requires the mediating, healing presence of a third party that can gather poem and poet into itself in a new unity. Something like the gathering into herself my mother does continually in my family. She is the on-going source of union for us. Centuries ago, the same dynamic led to the discovery that in God, too, there is a unitive being, a third. The very structure of our experience seems to be trinitarian. That third in God we call *Spirit*. The "spirit of health," in Hamlet's phrase, of healing, of oneness. The Father and the Son in effect both become mothers as a new, terrible, and hopeful life is torn from their conflict, their affection, and, finally, their loneliness to each other. Primordial Being. Expressive Being. Unitive Being. Ever at work on each other, in play with each other, keeping each other not only in being, but always fresh and interesting. The Son is the Word the Father speaks to his own temptation to suicide. The Spirit is God's own motherhood, as she chooses again in each instant to live.

The traditional description of the relatedness of God in terms of *Trinity* is more important than we are likely to acknowledge these days. At the very least, it indicates the futility of trying to talk about God in purely masculine terms. When the early church affirmed that the Third Person of the Trinity proceeds from the First Person and the Second Person together, and not from the First Person alone, it presumed a feminine principle in the

Godhead. The fact that the Second Person is called "Son," owing to incarnation in time as a male human being, Jesus, does not preclude the feminine character of its relationship to the First Person. The ancient instinct that God's being must be described by means of the full male-female analogy of human life was inadequately developed in that patriarchal age. But the notion of the Trinity itself represents an opening for contemporary theology in its effort to articulate the mystery of God in feminine as well as masculine terms. Orthodoxy holds that there is a kind of family life in God. Therefore our own family life, which is the basic human experience of relatedness, should also be seen as an image of transcendence.

In contrast to unitarian or polytheistic thinking, the notion of Trinity allows the tension of existence to have its place. Trinity prizes the tension between loneliness and communal intimacy, between person and nature, the many and the one. We are not pressed to the point of excommunication, of having to say "This and *not* that!" —of having to say, "Get out of church!" "Get out of God-head!" or, in the case of one's family, "Get out of the house!" Trinity is the proclamation that conflict makes the story memorable, whether it is the story of God or the story of one's people. There is no grace without polarity. The polarity of God takes flesh and we find that we are, as Jesus said, "alone, yet not alone" (John 16:32). We are belief and unbelief. We live on the edges of family, church, society, yet can claim to be of their very centers. *Margin-alization,* as sociologists call it, occurs when the tension is broken. The opposite of marginalization is *recovery,* the conversation that the edge maintains with its own center. *Trinity* proclaims that God is recovery itself, and that the principle of recovery, healing, and communion is implanted in the very structures of the universe.

Through the conversation, the tension that creature shares with Creator, we can claim that God is a "child-changed" parent not only in relation to Jesus but in relation to each of us. As adult sons and daughters we are empowered to call him *Abba,* mother-father. We have power over him. It is the power of generation; our I AM calls forth God's I AM. It is the power of recovery; our marginalization calls forth God's grace. We are the Word of God uttered to each other and to ourselves. We share in Expressive Being; we are the poem God composes. Each of us, in himself or herself, is enough to keep God from marginalization, from falling off the page, from suicide.

It is the mystery of *Pieta*—God, victim of the self-destructive forces in his own creation, at rest in the cradle of a woman's arms. Of our arms. God destroys himself to remake himself in us. We are the Son and the Word and the Mother before whom the Father stands awed and respectful. God sees himself in us. In us he sees his own act of I AM and knows therefore that *He* is good. We reveal to God his own goodness; it is the act which we call "praise." We are what keeps God from divine self-doubt. It is all part of the life that we share with each other and with all creatures, having discovered ourselves to be, finally, the family of God.

Reading over this, I know that most of it is heresy, some of it is absurd, and all of it is true.

PART THREE
Consequences

‖8‖

Consecration

The consequence of familyhood with God is "consecration." Jesus said, "I consecrated myself so that they too
may be consecrated in truth" (John 17:19).

But isn't "consecration" just a leftover word from the
shelf in the sacristy? Consecrated virgins. Consecrated
bishops. Consecrated hosts. Consecrated fingers. Consecrated martyrs. It is like being asked to star in an Ingmar
Bergman movie: it's something that doesn't happen to us.
Consecration is the rite of the church by which one becomes
an instant and authentic relic forever. Going. Going. Gone.

But John suggests that consecration could also be what
happens to us when we take seriously our own experience,
the memory of Jesus, and the claims of our people. Consecration is what happens when the free and dangerous
act of I AM becomes the feature of one's life. Consecration
is what happens when conversion moves from silence to
word.

To be called by God is to wrestle with him. A conse-crated person has no choice but to struggle with the Holy One. In the flesh. Beyond the flesh. This may seem an impossible image for the priesthood or the institutional-ized religious life. But where the warm puppy love of affluent boredom and an insurance policy for eternity is substituted for conflict with God and on God's behalf, true consecration ceases.

God calls human beings to be in relationship with him-self in the same way that Jesus is. That is the chief way in which the Son changes the Father, for in the Son the Father becomes Father *of flesh,* the flesh of Jesus and of ourselves. It is by dwelling in that relationship of mutual influence and affection that we are consecrated.

Israel knew well that its relationship with God required struggle with—and, at times, resistance to—God. The Jewish Scriptures have a well-developed sense of the duty and responsibility of arguing with God. This emerges most clearly in the stories of Moses, Ezekiel, Jeremiah, Isaias, Elijah, Jonah, and Amos. All found themselves in the position not only of proclaiming God's Word to the people, but also of representing the people's experience to God, and even, on some occasions, of trying to change God's mind. Because they were consecrated, made holy, they had the kind of intimate relationship with the Lord in which boldness and straightforwardness were not only allowed but required.

So, for example, the Lord says to Jeremiah: "Before you came to birth I consecrated you" (Jer. 1:5). And immediately Jeremiah dares to contradict the Lord, in effect refusing the honor: "Ah, Lord, Yahweh, look, I do not know how to speak. I am a child" (1:6). I'm not skilled enough, not man enough, to do your work, to be that close to you.

But the Lord insists: "Then Yahweh put out his hand and touched my mouth and said to me, 'There, I am putting my words into your mouth. Look, today I am setting you over nations and over kingdoms, to tear up and to knock down, to destroy and to overthrow, to build and to plant' " (1:9-10).

This commission to challenge, given in a time, like our own, of crumbling tradition, led Jeremiah eventually into real conflict with God. Again and again Jeremiah objected to the violence of God's ways with his people. He spoke what seemed to him to be the truth, despite its risks: "You have right on your side, Yahweh, when I complain about you. But I would like to debate a point of justice with you. Why is it that the wicked live so prosperously? Why do scoundrels enjoy peace? How long will the land be in mourning over their wickedness?" As if to say Jeremiah hadn't seen anything yet, God replies: "If you find it exhausting to race against men on foot how will you compete against horses?" (12:1-5). But Jeremiah goes on to accuse God: "Have you rejected Judah altogether? Does your very soul revolt at Zion?" (14:19). To which God replies in his impatience: Look, Jeremiah! "Even if Moses and Samuel were standing with you I could not warm to this people. Drive them out of my sight! Get them out of here!" (15:1-2). And Jeremiah, still resisting, snaps: "Lord, you are no better than a dried-up riverbed when the` people need water!" (15:18). Of course, if it gets serious, God wins. He blasts Jeremiah for his "despicable thoughts" (15:19), orders him against his will to live a life of celibacy (16:1).

It was the instinct of the people of Israel that God, unlike those frightened leaders who surround themselves with yes men, welcomes the fight. He wants to be child-changed. Ezekiel has God make the extraordinary admission that he does, now and then, go overboard in punishing the people. But often, God says, it is the fault of the prophet for not arguing him out of it. Indeed, beyond mere arguing, God wants human beings to stand in his way and stop him when, in his anger, he tries to storm the walled city. "Like jackals in a ruin, so are you, prophets of Israel." It is God who speaks: "You have never ventured into the breach. You have never bothered to fortify the House of Israel, to hold fast in battle on the Day of Yahweh" (Ezek. 13:5). You are scavengers, sniffing in ruins, hypnotized by defeat.

God consecrates human beings to stand in his presence and say I AM, to step in his way, to say as Isaias did, pointing to the ravaged city, "Lord, can you go unmoved by all of this, oppressing us beyond measure by your silence?" (Isa. 64:12). Moses stands before God, who is outraged at the idolatry of the golden calf, and protests, "How can you wipe out the entire people?"

In Jesus our expectations of God change, but the meaning of "consecration" does not. The one whom we call *Abba* is not the perverse, whimsical oppressor against whom the prophets rebel. He is the source of life and being itself, with whom we are in a relationship of tension and contention toward the future. He is the *Abba* whose I AM teaches us the duty always to represent the experience of "flesh" to the "spirit," the experience of the people to God. Consecration is the call to stand in the breach of God's silence, saying I AM, whether God is or not. One rises to face God's absence with one's own presence, saying I AM HERE, regardless. God drafts us for this dreadful mission so that in us he might speak and might be present. In some way we enable God to exist. Consecrated, we move into the future, which is unknown to us and therefore to God. We are made holy in order to be his flesh, his Word, his outrage, and his embrace of whatever comes. The purpose of life, Kilgore Trout says in Vonnegut's *Breakfast of Champions,* is "to be the eyes and ears and conscience of the creator of the universe" (p. 67).

The disciples of Jesus, consecrated in Word and in truth, are to be listeners, speakers, bearers of God's Word. We join our own destinies to the adventures of the Word in its terrible movement from silence to flesh. To speak God's Word is the ultimate act of I AM—one's own being and the being of God become joined not only at some preconscious level of existence but also in the very chosen purpose of one's life. One lives to be the mouth of God. Aware of the sacredness of its mission, "consciousness," says Dostoevsky, "kindled by the will of a higher power, has turned round upon the world and said I AM."

The consecration of Isaias was sealed by a live coal pressed to his mouth. When the fire cooled, the Lord said, "Whom shall I send? Who will be our messenger?" And Isaias replied, "Here I AM! Send me!" (Isa. 6:7-8).

And what was he sent to do? Isaias describes the mission of the consecrated one in language that is familiar because Jesus recognized in it a description of his own mission: "The breath of the Lord has been given to me for he has consecrated me. He has sent me to bring good news to the poor, to bind up hearts that are broken, to proclaim liberty to captives, and to the blind new sight, to proclaim the Lord's year of favor, to comfort all those who mourn. They will rebuild the ancient ruins. They will raise what has long lain waste. They will restore the ruined cities. For I, the Lord, love justice!" (Isa. 61:1-2; Mark 4:17-20).

We are consecrated, finally, to be servants of justice, agents of our people. Justice has become the very name of God. In fact, the only expression Jesus uses of God besides the *Abba* in the prayer of John 17 is "Just One" (17:25). It is the concrete version of the abstract name of God, the I AM in relation to human beings, to flesh. The word itself means standing upright, which is why it is often translated in older texts as "righteousness" or "uprightness." When a man or a woman *stands up,* as we have seen, it is not simply a personal act of liberation, not just a private victory over suicide. It is an act of political affirmation that sends waves of influence, if not shock, through the corrupt and corrupting structures of society.

That is why the encounter with the world involves *conflict.* It is more than a matter of spitting in the eye of existential anxiety. The "Evil One" has endless resources, jails, armies, weapons—not to mention electronic bugging equipment—as well as a bottomless pool of protected indifference, witty conversation, and snobbish disregard for ordinary people. To step out of that lockstep, to do more than regret "the way things are"; to step into the life-and-death struggle that goes on in the old neighborhoods and new suburbs, to enter the very pit of chaos, and in one's own name and in the name of all humanity, to open one's mouth and make the poor, battered universe resound with the cry I AM—that is consecration.

In our time this magnificent and dreadful calling has taken on very specific meanings. Events and persons have altered some of our most traditional notions. As Rosemary Ruether has pointed out, for example, "in the monastic spirituality of Thomas Merton traditional Christian rejection of 'this world' took on a new and concrete meaning not as a struggle against the flesh and blood, but as a struggle against the powers and principalities of the great empires, with America as their most recent representative" ("Monks and Marxists," *Christianity and Crisis,* 30 April 1973, p. 221).

We have come a long way from the usual institutional view that limits consecration to virgins and eunuchs and makes its condition the habit of submission and the hope of self-obliteration. The Scriptures speak, rather, of an immense struggle with the unspeakable fears and the hidden monsters that live in us and beyond us. It is not that indignation or violence should become our new deities, though we know the struggle can be deadly. It is a combat that we hope, perhaps absurdly, will end in embrace, will be, in its deepest part, an ocean of embrace. For didn't Rilke tell us that "everything terrible is in *its* deepest part only something helpless wanting help from us."

The wrestling of which the Scriptures speak is not only with God as adversary, but with God as partner, as together we draw order and meaning and justice from the chaos-pit that seethes within us. For we must finally come to recognize that consecration is responsibility for history. To withdraw from the frontier where history tears itself from the flesh of humanity is to forfeit consecration. Even when the withdrawal occurs in the name of religion. Especially when the withdrawal occurs in the name of religion.

We are consecrated to a kind of radicalism that "seeks

to place the individual in that ultimate clash between good and evil which is the boundary situation of human history" (Ruether, "Monks and Marxists," p. 223). The radicalism we seek tries to avoid arrogance and cruelty because, Jesus says, we are "consecrated in truth." We hope to speak the truth in whatever way we can. But we do not kill for it, or hate in its name, or excommunicate our opponents because we do not own it. Indeed, we do not *have* truth; in Gabriel Marcel's distinction, the truth *has us.* It owns us. The Word we speak does not belong to us; we belong to it.

"Truth? What is truth?" Pilate asks. And Jesus replies only with his life, having already declared, "I am the truth." In making his "good profession," he uncovers for us the first and last implication of consecration: death. To live this way, exposed, out of the trench, standing, vulnerable, ready to move, to change and resist is, finally, to die. That is why we all do it so poorly.

In the memory of Israel prophets were not the only ones who were consecrated. The victims of sacrifice were consecrated too. "You must consecrate every first-born male from your herd and flock to Yahweh your God" (Deut. 15:19). When Jesus says, "I consecrate myself" (John 17:19), it has precisely the same meaning, according to Raymond Brown (*Anchor Bible,* 29:765), as when he says, "I lay down my life" (John 10:17). Jesus takes responsibility for his own death. It becomes his act of I AM. Death is the consequence of his standing up. We return to an act of self-killing. Jesus is not a passive victim of forces outside his control. "No one takes my life from me. I lay it down of my own accord" (John 10:18). *He* lays his life down. He consecrates himself.

But there is an enormous difference between his act and the I AM NOT of suicide. Suicide is not consecration for two reasons, both given by Jesus himself. The first is that the consecration of death is an act for others: "For their sake I consecrate myself" (John 17:16); "A man lays down his life for his friends" (10:10); "I lay down my life for my sheep" (10:15). Jesus never allows himself the narcissistic luxury of seeing his conflict in terms of self against all others. He consistently portrays the conflict as with the "Evil One." He gives himself to the struggle precisely *for* all others. His death is not simply the vindication of his own I AM, but of the I AM of all creation. All others share in his victory over I AM NOT. Jesus creates death; he does not identify with it. He creates death for all of us, unlike the suicide who, even as scapegoat for the enormous anxieties of our age, creates death for the self alone.

Jesus avoids the self-mockery of suicide in another way as well, by embracing destruction only in order to create himself anew, in and with and for others; "I lay down my life in order to take it up again" (John 10:17). Jesus goes into death in order to change it. He is not interested in "enduring everything," nor is he interested in the role of the lonely hero. What we call "resurrection-glorification" is the transformation of death from a momentary burden borne alone to a permanent burden shared. Because it is shared, the nature of the burden changes; it *remains* burden, but it becomes burden-to-life.

We are the ones with whom Jesus shares the burden. We are the condition of its transformation. In us Jesus returns to the Father, not alone, but in the solidarity of flesh. Now our burden is transfigured, though never removed. Those who claim that Easter removes the burden

of death practice a kind of paschal magic. We build a
life around a mystery, not magic. Death clings to us and
our fate is always heavy with its coming. But because we
are consecrated, we have a Word to speak to the silence
that tugs at us even now. "We have been consecrated
through the offering of the body of Jesus Christ once for
all" (Heb. 10:10).

The consecration we share is not bestowed on us individually, as if we had been privately sent forth by God.
We are together made a consecrated community.

Obviously, the notion of community is difficult to value
today, bearing as it does all the weight of contemporary
disorder. We are increasingly aware of the lack of shared
values and beliefs that have traditionally defined community. And so we find ourselves drawn into the easy yet
macabre pastime of berating our various connections with
each other. Loving criticism so easily slides into nit-picking,
cynicism, and even hatred of the very people who make
us what we are.

The scriptures, however, call us to serve the common
life that we share with each other, to "rebuild the ruined
city." In the Bible that common life does not depend on
all the things we usually identify with it—shared goals,
language, assumptions. Today we must relearn this lesson,
that community exists not because of any human construction but because we all share in the I AM of God.

Community is not something we work toward to build
or organize. It simply is. Community is the reality uncovered by Jesus Christ in his proclamation that the heart of
the universe is appropriately called *Abba*. In *that* bond we
can hope to go beyond even the definitions of family to
a communion of persons whose kinship is a matter not

of blood, class, nation, or history, but simply of a shared act of existence.

The act of I AM that we each discover in ourselves implies, as William Chaplin observes, the continual "agony of reconstructing a world out of our separate existences" (*American Poetry Review* 2, no. 3 [1973]: 52). It implies *standing up* alone, on one's own two feet, upright, on one's own piece of earth. But that solitary standing is in itself an act of communion pointing to a lasting solidarity.

I think of the drama enacted in Leonard Bernstein's *Mass*. When the meaning of the ritual and the words explode in the terrible breakdown of the celebrant, the several hundred singers, dancers, players, prayers all fall down, alone, disillusioned, failed, demythologized, declericalized, dead. We recognize the feeling at once. We have been there. We have been on the floor of that vast valley of dry bones that Ezekiel saw when he looked in himself and at his people. As Sylvia Plath said in "Daddy," "I thought even the bones would do." But they don't. All you have to do is try staying in bed for one whole day, pretending your sickness is of the body. The bones won't do. So you try going to the movies, though it is afternoon. But the bones won't do. And the choice becomes clearer and clearer.

What we need is for the Word, in its shuttle between silence and flesh, to pause over *our* dullness. Over *our* disillusionment with each other. Over *our* preference for an abstract perfection instead of people as they are, since that is what kills us. We need the Word that will call breath from the four winds to breathe in *us*—as *we* are. To get blood moving in our sinews and skin, to get muscles aching and joints cracking in the embarrassment of standing to someone else's act of I AM. It can be God's or a young boy's, as it is in the *Mass* by Bernstein.

But the I AM is contagious. If at first it is a noise, "a sound of clattering," soon it becomes a pure, joyous song of delight: "The breath entered them and they came to life again and stood on their feet, and they were a great and immense people" (Ezek. 37:10).

Holy Father, Jesus prayed, *keep those you have given me true to your name so that they may be one like us* (John 17:11). To be one like they are, we recall, is to be "alone, but not really alone." As Bernstein remembers the moment we all share, the young boy finds it in himself to stand. He is alone; everyone else is on the floor, Then, softly, gently, his gaze wakens someone else. His act of standing alone calls forth another act of fidelity to God's name. A dancer stands, alone. The boy and the dancer, in the same movement, stand toward each other. They exchange the ancient kiss of peace, which goes through the dead throng like a wind, like God's breath. A whole succession of solitary acts of I AM follow upon each other as men and women stand, exchange the kiss, and the ancient imposition of hands. They thereby claim again their common consecration—to be healers of selves, discoverers of freshness, sharing in the building of a new world out of separate existences.

And they sing: "You can lock up the bold ones, but you cannot imprison the Word of the Lord." And they are again a great and immense people.

It could be the story of the human race today. It could be the story of the church. It could be the story of me and my four brothers. A couple of years ago, visiting the old house in which we'd lived as children and to which Mom and Dad had returned after retirement, Joe, the psychologist, Brian, the agent, and I walked into the woods down the road. We found without trouble the grand oak in which we'd built our tree house. It had been a massive and elaborate design, an architect's dream, a fort, a plateau, a tower—everything you could want when you were seven, ten, and twelve. But finding it again that December Sunday afternoon, all we could see was a few meager boards barely hanging on to the first large branch. It had not been so much. Not enough to live in forever, though as kids we had thought it might be. The three of us laughed once together, fell quiet, and then left quickly. Whatever it had been, it was not what we shared anymore.

But what we share is more trustworthy, finally, than a few boards, or even an explicit articulation of common values. We share an act of I AM inherited from an Irish past that exploded in time in the loving flesh of a good man and a good woman. As each of us builds a different life in a different place in a different way, we are still all trying to be faithful to that one act. We have been afflicted with similar tastes for nothingness, and truthfulness comes no easier to us than to others, but our common life not only survives diversity but thrives on it.

This is true for all our communities, or could be. The act of I AM alone sustains relationship. The healing Word of God is implanted in our life together. A sense of the One Life we share must inform all our choices. It survives our wars, our disillusionments, our unbelief. It is the basis for our claim that there is another way to live than killing. Human life itself is consecration to that hope. Out of what is elemental to our common act of being we affirm what is transcendent.

We know all too well how we fail each other and ourselves, infected as we are with the clinging spirit of nihilism. The boards of our meager house are nailed, almost literally, to the flesh and bones of other men and women. Their hunger is what feeds us. Such is the grip of the "Evil One" on us that, even knowing the suicidal wages of our sin, we resist so poorly. "That's what evil is," says Kate to her pathetic husband in William Alfred's *Hogan's Goat,* "the starvation of a nothing heart that makes the world around it nothing too."

In the face of such knowledge as *that,* we still find it in ourselves to stand. We stand alone. We stand together. We say no to our nothing heart and meet each other in the ancient kiss of peace. The offer of forgiveness. The demand for truth. "We must love each other or die," writes W. H. Auden. The consecration we share consists of being alive at a time of high danger. It is not a consecration of oil or "prayer," of custom or inheritance. It is a consecration of silence and of fire.

‖ 9 ‖

With Jesus

The last words of Jesus, according to John 17, are "that I may be in them." The last words of his prayer remind us of the extraordinary claims our shared memory makes. From the earliest days of the tradition it has been proclaimed that Jesus, the man, the person of God, lives with and in his followers.

My earlier question now bubbles to the surface. After a season of turning him over like a last coin, after looking for the changed name of God and coming up with as much or as little as "freshness," "Justice," or "I AM," what do I believe about Jesus? Do I believe that he is "in me"? "In us"? Or is that one more piece of dropsical piety abandoned to the valley of lost beliefs outside the city?

It's a problem. Clearly, the memory of Jesus is important to me. I would not have been swinging around the pole of his last words all summer if it weren't. I wouldn't have buried myself in this Latin Mass of a monastery (I'm tired of the place, frankly) somewhere between Beth-

lehem and Jerusalem. I have been here trying to find out
what clings to me of belief. What do I cling to? And what
about Jesus?

It will surely be amazing if my old belief that Jesus
is somehow "in me" survives. *All* aspects of belief in Jesus
are in serious jeopardy, both peripheral and central ones,
partly because the pressures of our age are so hostile
toward them, and partly because the "protectors" of the
tradition, the churches, seem so set on suicide. For a
person of religious sensibility to maintain a vital connection with both today's broken world and the spiritual
claims of the past, an immense and isolated act of discipline is required. No one ever said, of course, that it was
easy to move through a mutation of history. It takes less
effort to become fossilized.

One of the barriers to my getting to know Jesus and
to believe in him as "in me" has been his sudden popular-
ity the last few years. Perhaps it will prove to be as temporary as it appears to be shallow. The well-scrubbed
piety which continually invokes the name of Jesus makes
me want to deny ever having had anything to do with him.
He has been converted into another fourteen-year-old
Maharaj Ji, only older and Jewish. The fact that the
counter-cultural style of the piety has been embraced
both by the cynics of commerce ("it sells records") and
by the cynics of religion ("it gets the kids back") can
make it embarrassing to be a Christian. What will I do
if some pigtailed, pink-cheeked stranger pops out from
behind my meager act of faith, kisses me, and gives me
a pocket Bible?

Is Jesus present in me? In us? It would hardly seem so,
at least in any of the ways in which we had been accus-

tomed to talk about it. Much of the imagery of Jesus' presence to his people is bankrupt. The good words from Scripture have consistently been abandoned. Paul talks about the community as the "body" of Christ, for example. But the body in our time is something we deny through false pieties or idolize through center-fold hedonism. Authentic metaphors of belief increasingly elude us. We are not dealing simply with a private crisis of faith in Jesus. We are the products of a community whose blind commitment to a "doctrine" of Jesus has led it to effectively deny his reality.

I do not believe in the triumphal, imperial kingship of Jesus. His "glory" and "majesty" mean nothing to me if they must be interpreted in the language of a class system that leaves the majority dispossessed. There is a centuries-old piety that insists that the meaning of Jesus has to do with royalty, power, and victory. Such a conception makes him into a kind of benign Caesar and, by more than coincidence, helps to justify all those other Caesars, political and ecclesial, who are anything but benign.

Nor do I believe in the Jesus who glides, singing, over a tepid ocean of good feelings. He was neither the first hippie nor Young Werther. He was not Young Love either, or even Saint Francis. If Jesus' presence in my life simply testifies to my need to avoid conflict, I can as readily turn to liquor and dope, both of which have their risks but don't require that I be stupid.

"Compared to fantasy, love is a harsh and dreadful thing," writes Dostoevsky. I believe *that*. Jesus has little to do with our pastel fantasies or with the calculated inarticulateness that masquerades as innocence. Not that

Jesus was some kind of humorless Marxist. Or, indeed, a "revolutionary." God save the revolution from the "revolutionaries." I don't know whether Jesus would wear Ben Franklin glasses, if he had bad eyes, or horned rims. I don't care.

Whatever our personal piety, it must not violate the central fact of our belief about Jesus: incarnation. Incarnation means that the man Jesus was utterly indistinguishable from other men of his community. He was flesh, as we are. A good man, no doubt. Free from sin, perhaps, but not, in any case, from its effects. There was nothing about him which set him apart from, much less above, the other rabbis and wandering teachers of his time. Not even his "holiness" or "perfection." Ironically, his holiness contributed widely to his public image as a suspect character who kept "bad company." If a faith in Jesus is to survive into the new age, we must tone down our rhetoric and claim less for him. In other words, we must learn to think of Jesus and speak of him more or less the way he did himself.

There is a Jesus-idolatry that refuses to admit, much less worship, his fleshiness. I'm not referring only to the churchly idolatry that emphasized his divinity to the all-but-exclusion of his humanity. We must also oppose the widespread idealization of Jesus that claims to love his humanity but in effect denies it by confusing his flesh with cotton candy. The hippie Jesus is no more a human being than the caesaro-papal version was.

At the basis of all forms of Jesus-idolatry is the inability or refusal to see that the most intense conflict of Jesus' existence was conflict with himself. The issue in Jesus' life was *his* choice between *his* I AM and *his* I AM NOT.

Beginning with his first followers, that struggle has been
objectified, intellectualized, and spiritualized so that now
we think of it as Jesus' conflict with extrinsic enemies—
the "Evil One," "the world," or "the Jews." The effects
of the refusal to locate the conflict of Jesus precisely *within*
his manhood have been disastrous. To take only one
example, the most shameful, the Christian impulse to
spiritualize Jesus led even in New Testament times to an
emphasis on external enemies as the source of Jesus'
trouble. In our day this is known as the old "outside agita-
tor" dodge: avoid facing the enemy within by finding
one outside.

The external enemy *par excellence,* of course, has always
been the Jews. Never mind that in New Testament times
this ignores the fact that Jesus was in conflict with himself
long before the conflict became political and focused on
the authorities. Equally important is the fact that right
to the end of his life Jesus remained an observant Jew
for whom Israel was ever the sign of God's love for the
world. Jews were no more the source of Jesus' conflict
than communists were the source of conflict at Kent State.
The followers of Jesus consistently do to themselves precisely what they did to Jesus: they objectify their own
inner conflict, directing their rage and hostility toward an
external enemy. More often than not, the Jews. Nazism
sprang from the soil prepared for it by Christianity—
by, it should be emphasized, a complete misunderstanding
of who Jesus was. Should we be surprised that Hitler's
demand that Jews wear the yellow Star of David had
earlier been imposed by the Lateran Council of the Catholic Church?

When we see the conflict Jesus describes between himself and "the world" as a conflict within the self, suicide becomes a crucial metaphor because it demonstrates that the "Evil One" exists precisely as the enemy within. This is certainly the perspective of John, who understands the conflict of Jesus as being between the levels of existence he confronts in himself and not between two separate orders of existence, one good and one bad. John has a respect for the complexity of incarnation and he maintains his commitment to keeping the poles of the struggle related to each other in the unity of the human existence of Christ. (It should be recognized, however, that owing apparently to the circumstances of the Johannine community by the end of the first century, the Gospel of John clearly casts "the Jews" in the role of villain. Of course, there is no reason to deny that Jesus and his followers were in conflict with some Jews, but any reading of that conflict that focuses on the Jewishness of Jesus' adversaries ignores Jesus' own Jewishness and perverts the meaning of the deeper human conflict in what, as history teaches, has been a most murderous way.)

In Jesus' prayer, the use of the term "Evil One" should be seen in the context of the temptation stories, both the earlier scene in the desert and the later one in the garden of Gethsemane. Whatever one thinks of the "Evil One," whether as a separate personal being or a metaphorical image for evil forces, clearly the *experience* Jesus has is of intense personal wrestling with himself. The wonder and mystery of incarnation is that God enters the common, polarized flesh of a human being. Whatever I can believe about Jesus must be rooted in *that* sense about him. To have this intense desire to cling to Jesus is to recognize him as one who shares our experience of conflict and

commonness. And to recognize him as one who responds
to his experience with such a powerful act of creativity
that we know that we are capable of it too.

The key to belief in him, as we have seen repeatedly
by now, is the *Abba* of Jesus. Again, what makes Jesus
unique is the discovery in himself of the communion with
Being Itself that he describes in terms of that word. Apparently the most important thing about Jesus to his
own mind was his sense of being the only Son of the
Father. "*Abba* represents the center of Jesus' awareness
of his mission," notes Joachim Jeremias (*Central Message*,
p. 27).

If belief in Jesus is to mean anything more than institutionalized compulsion or hippie-love, it must confront
this claim Jesus makes about himself. I have interpreted
the claim in terms of the I AM of God. Is that good
enough? Does that water down what Jesus claims? In what
way does Jesus mean God is his *Abba*? Is it mere metaphor?
But what is *mere* metaphor anyway?

For John, according to Raymond Brown (*Anchor
Bible*, 29:751), "To believe in Jesus is to adhere to the
dogma of his relationship with the Father." Perhaps dogma
is what happens when you get so far inside the truth you
forget what it looks like as a whole and then can't get
out to see it. When you focus on the meaning of the
language you use, it's hard sometimes to remember what
the language refers to. In the final analysis, is all my talk
about Jesus anything more than poetry? I don't mean
mere poetry—I love poetry. In fact I would never muddy
it up with religion unless I had to. The question is, do
I have to? Is the *Abba* of Jesus the *Abba* of Jesus? The
answer for me is simple; I don't quite know.

Ambiguity can be a frantic ride on the furthest edge of a violent ocean wave that wrecks itself on the rugged coast of an undiscovered continent. It can also be ambiguity.

Dogma exists to help us cope with ambiguity when it is only ambiguity. I cling to the language about Jesus that is in the lively center of my people's memory about him *because* it is in that center. In these pages I have been trying to make some sense of this language. Perhaps in the discovery of freshness in and beyond experience, particularly the experiences of sonship and life in chaos, I have not altogether failed. If my headache won't let me claim the "dogma" easily as my own, neither am I ready to dismiss the memory, the language, and the faith profession of two thousand years. *I believe in God, the Father Almighty, Creator of Heaven and earth, and in Jesus Christ his only Son, our Lord.*

"You are the Christ, the Son of the Living God." If it had been an easy profession to make, Jesus would not have made Peter Pope when he did it. What we need are pairs of fresh ears with which to hear the old words. For example, these of Irenaeus: "He who is uncomprehensible, intangible, and invisible has made himself seen and grasped and understood by men so that those who understand and see him may live. . . . The only life is participation in God and we do this by knowing God and enjoying his goodness" *(Against Heresy,* IV 20:5). Suddenly the question is no longer how to make sense of the two thousand years but how to be worthy of them.

But the argument with myself goes on. Mind and the need to speak require that I locate my experiences in belief of some specificity. The faith of the Christian people gives me a story in terms of which I can tell my own. The life and death of Jesus in history root that story in a shared act of remembering. The continuing life and death of Jesus in glory make that story available to me. Jesus' continuing life as Word of the Father means that my experience of the creative word I AM, whether of poetry or of love, is a revelation to me of God. The whole point of everything is to uncover God's life in one's own life. By faithfully following the adventures of the Word, my progress back and forth between silence and flesh becomes God's life in mine.

I think of lingering over breakfast. Even here, at the monks' house, one of my dearest pleasures is to savor the beginning of the day. Usually the monks eat in silence and rush off to their duties, while I sit there having more coffee. I make small talk with myself, look out the window, watch dust particles rising with the sun, and enjoy the smell of freshness, the sound of desert creatures coming to life. I sit for a few moments most mornings in the middle of delight itself. It is hardly a major event, and probably not profound. It is the simplest joy I know.

If I relish the memory of Jesus, it is because he makes his home amid such thoroughly ordinary moments. He does not build a life of greatness, importance, ultimacy. As I remember him, what Jesus mainly does is eat, linger at the table with people. All kinds of people. I see Jesus sitting there, not being rushed, making small talk with whoever cares to join in. There is an ease, a relaxation, a uselessness at the heart of Jesus' life, and that is what I treasure most in my own.

All this is not to question the need of transcendence.

But I do not know how to speak of it if not in terms of Jesus. My memory of him as a man "in bad company" enables me to see my wrestling, rebellion, and even dishonesty and prejudice, as a preparation for—indeed condition of—relationship with God. My memory of Jesus as a friend of sinners gives me a way *presently* of living with *my* sin, neither denying it nor surrendering to it. The memory of Jesus as a troubled man prepared me for trouble. If he somehow lives on in me, I might yet dare to embrace the trouble that acts of truthfulness and affirmation always seem to bring with them.

I prize John's memory of Jesus as a polarized man who constantly struggles to maintain the tension of a deeper unity. The ambiguity and paradox that fascinate, yet threaten to paralyze, were in him too. So he could say in the course of his prayer, "I am no longer in the world" (John 17:11), and "While still in the world" (17:13). Exactly. I don't know where I am half the time either. From this perspective, the resurrection of Jesus in glory becomes the act of perfect tension, the exquisite balance that I seek as the ultimate sign of God's presence. The tension broken is a sure sign of his absence, of the I AM NOT, as the old legal definition of suicide implies: "death by one's own hand while the balance of one's mind is disturbed." Thus survival of one's own oppositions is not merely survival. It has the meaning of grace and carries the promise that there is a survival, even of death. It all comes down to dying, as did the life of Jesus.

Because this man is glorified in crucifixion, we can admit the suffering in our lives and can experience it as transformed into something that is never easy, but is full of meaning. The continued glory of Jesus in us is the act of sharing burdens. He shares ours. And more, we share his. The burden of Jesus does not kill him because even now he shares it with each of us. That is why the glory of Jesus depends not only on the loving fatherhood of God, but on you and me, and other taggers-along. As he says to God, "All I have is yours and all you have is mine, and *in them* I am glorified" (John 17:10).

The movement goes both ways. Though its implications are impossible to appreciate fully, the relationship we followers claim to have with Jesus is one of equality, of brotherhood/sisterhood, of mutually refreshing love. We keep each other going. In the prayer John records, the Jesus of this love emerges clearly in the simple concern and affection he has for the human beings with whom he had walked the road from Bethlehem to Jerusalem. He is worried about them. "Protect them . . . keep them . . . consecrate them . . . be with them." Jesus is one of them. "For their sake . . . I pray for them . . . they are mine." And he is one of those who follow after them. "May they be one in us. . . . May the love with which you loved me be in them so that I may be in them." This is not puppy love. It is the harsh affection a man feels for the friends who share his burden. That Passover night it was the burden of an imminent death. Now it is the burden of a world that groans in the agony of giving birth to itself. However remotely or imperfectly, we Christians claim his burden as our own. The glory is in our partnership through Jesus with God.

This partnership is the privilege that comes of being "chosen," "elected," special. Israel discovered in itself the sense that this transcendent act of affection is so extra-ordinary and gratuitous that it could only be the result of God's free choice. And so the Jews understood themselves as chosen.

Because Jesus is a Jew I can claim that election as my own. I am not a Jew and would not presume to claim to be, but in Jesus I do have a special relationship with God. I am one of God's people through adoption, as Paul says, not by inheritance. Suddenly the magnificent story of the children of Abraham is mine, if only indirectly. God acts in and through the history of people. Of my people. And in Jesus I understand that that election means I can address the transcendent other as *Abba.* And there is the further discovery that God acts in and through my history as a man.

It is not just that the religious genius of the chosen people becomes mine as I too am chosen. Nor that God lives in me through Israel and Jesus as one of his special ones. But that *every human being is chosen of God.* Of course, if we really believed that there would be no war, for war requires the assumption that only one's own group is the chosen one. In Jesus I understand what I never would have come to see otherwise, that all people are God's special ones. No matter what they do or say, religiously or otherwise. I make no claim about myself as one of God's chosen that is not true of every human being—Jew, Gentile, Arab, Italian, Vietnamese, and FBI. All the earth is the household of God.

After everything is said, it is a matter of deciding how one will interpret his experience. Do I decide to see transcendence at the heart of engagement? Do I decide to speak to that transcendence and hear it speak to me in the words proposed by the life and model of Jesus? Do I want to continue to think of myself as a believer?

These days of living on the land over which he walked have taught me one thing: it is possible for me to learn myself in terms of Jesus. It is possible for me to make sense to myself about myself by struggling with my memory of Jesus and with the claims my people make in his name. That is not nothing. I have not committed suicide, and the language of transcendence offers me a way of saying why.

But how do I know who Jesus was? How do I know whether or not he lives in me? Who do people say he is?

I don't know. I can only answer with what I say to everything that is precious and beautiful and urgent in my life: I'm not sure. But Jesus responds the way an honest lover would: "That's not enough, sweetheart. Be for or against." And I know again that the only way out of my deadly but ever-so-liberal idolatry of the question itself is an answer.

And so I give one, take one. Yes. Yes. Yes.

Are you surprised? Did you think I would take you all this way to report on what I reject? Well, I would have, if it had come to that; I have been after the truth. The trouble is that, as Pilate told us, truth is quite complex. In the end truth may be at least partly involved with what you make it to be.

And so I say yes. I believe in Jesus Christ living in me, or however the dogma at the center of our memory puts it. I am not unaware of the irony. I decide for Jesus and the universe resounds with the cry, "So what?" In fact, in large part, so do I. That must be because deciding to live one's life in the light of *that* Word is a matter of much more than sitting alone at a monk's desk on a windy summer night in Israel. Frankly, not much seems to change. No lightning. No heavens opening. I suspect that God himself would be just as happy if I decided to be an honest atheist. I'm afraid he'll have to settle for my decision to continue as a more or less dishonest Christian. Since I'm Irish, I doubt that he is surprised.

I have not been deciding for or against just Jesus. It has also been a matter of deciding what community I claim as my own. That has its ironies, of course, as well. Looking at the church now is like standing under the big, old tree of your youth and being amazed that a few meager boards had once seemed magnificent. Amazed that a tree house could have seemed to be a cathedral. And amazed that such a human construction could provoke such anger in one's breast. I have been looking at the church, and, for all its meagerness, rusty nails, and clinging structures, I recognize it as my own.

The difficulty in the fact that the choice for Jesus implies membership in the community of those who follow him is that right now it is impossible to say what that means. So much about the church is unclear. Perhaps our moment is something like the moment of the Reformation. When a massive shift is occurring, it is impossible to say exactly where one is. Two things seem clear, though. One is that as long as I choose to interpret my life in terms of the life of Jesus, I am in the church. As long as he lives for me, I will not leave the church. The church is how I remain in touch with his Word and its ever-changing meaning. I need the challenge, the forgiveness, and the nurture of the church. I do not intend to be a sect of one, or even of several hundred.

I am also certain that the church is in the midst of a massive cultural and religious realignment. I dearly hope that what the world knows and some of us love as the *Catholic* church will survive this period, purified, ready to live again at the service of justice. But it may also turn out that the *Catholic* church, in its freedom, may have chosen to sit down on the arctic tundra and die of its false dignity.

If so, as Jesus said, it can bury itself. But the confessing movement will go on, gathering and being gathered. The church will live in a new way, with new meanings, new power centers, new symbols for its life in common. We cannot predict its shape, but it will still come together to confess the name of Jesus and to make known and available to those who seek his discovery of *Abba* at the heart of all existence. In simplicity and renewed acts of belief, we will continue to share in Christ's yearning for our deliverance so that he can be in us fully.

Prayer

The church is nothing if not the gathering of people for the purpose of prayer. The consecration I claim for myself is nothing if not the consecration to prayer.

But by now we are used to thinking this is not the time for prayer. By now we are all familiar with the embarrassment that comes of the misuse of prayer, our own and other people's. Before glibly pronouncing this a time for prayer, one must even more vigorously proclaim that this is a time for straining against the limits of our traditions and our laws and our habits in order to turn back the rising tide of violence. We must keep reminding ourselves that the only God worth believing in requires engagement with history as the first act of worship.

Because the times are marked by unparalleled indifference and moral paralysis, prayer itself is mocked by prevailing institutions and structures, even religious ones. Especially religious ones. This is the time when prayer is claimed to be the special possession of initiated people who pretend to be friends to prayer but are its enemy.

Partly because there is a grace to being out of joint with such times, we return to prayer. So it has been with me. In the final analysis, I have to admit that people are, above all, worshipers. I even begin to suspect that human beings know most about prayer when it is not easy. Prayer is, or can be, part of the lives of everyone, not only of those of monks and Greek hermits. But the great and ancient religious categories of silence, darkness of the soul, and ecstasy translate differently in our time. The holy solitude of the hermitage has its equivalent now in crowded assembly lines where men and women, though shoulder to shoulder, stand alone amid deafening noise and boredom for hours at a time. There is the silence of commuting, of going home in the new monk's cell—the automobile—with only the false conversation of a radio announcer. The night of the soul presses in on men and women who are exhausted to the point of sleeplessness by fears of assault on the street and wages too small to cover the bills. Minds burdened with the nearly infinite options of contemporary life and hearts filled with the demands of daily living that cruelly narrow those choices are too much to carry alone. And so, in their own fashion, at home, on the street, at work, at play, people lift their minds and hearts to the One who has promised to receive such common offerings.

We must discover or remember several things: prayer is not a special activity reserved to elites of any kind— clerical, charismatic, holy, or desperate. Prayer is the consequence in human beings of God's existence, of God's act of I AM. The convictions that prayer is important and that God exists are fragile, tenuous, and always in danger of being forgotten. The I AM is always at odds with the I AM NOT. There is a spiritual suicide and we are capable of it. Though this may not seem to be the time for prayer, we must act, for that reason, as if it were.

By now we know that prayer is a matter of solitude, of being alone with darkness and silence. And that prayer is a matter of communion, of being alive to the connections we share with creation in its fullness and emptiness, the connections we share with the people—mothers and fathers in faith—who have taught us how to worship, the connections we share with God in the divine life of communion we call *Trinity*.

We could go on. Prayer is this and prayer is that. Prayer is yes and no. Everything and nothing. Prayer is. But finally another question demands our attention. It is not a question about prayer, but about us.

What is prayer to *us*? What difference does it make in and to the lives we make alone and together? How does a prayerful person live? Just supposing for a moment that we do know what prayer is and that it is possible for us, what does it all mean on, let us say, a Tuesday in July, when our country is continuing its endless project of recovery from self-doubt? When our world bumps steadily along to dreadful places? When our careers go sour, or, happily, when friends surprise us with unexpected kindness? How does prayer affect us in our movement toward our own futures?

I am thinking of some "prayerful people" I know. One would never call them that to their faces, of course. Perhaps closer attention to their lives will tell us something for our own. They are not saints. Or monks. They are a cabby named Pat who loves driving in Boston, a class-

mate of mine who gives good parties, a China scholar
I know who makes great conversation, a college kid who
sells sandwiches on the sidewalk. None of them is particularly "holy." But they are people who sustain the
activity and attitude of mind and heart we hint at with
the word "prayer." They sustain it in themselves and
invite it in others.

I don't know the details of schedule or the habits of
worship of these people. I don't make the judgment that
they are prayerful because I know how or how often
or in what tongue they pray. I am thinking of them as
"prayerful" in the way we think of some people as truthful.
It is a matter not of detail but of spirit. It is a matter
of the tangible fashion in which their act of I AM is
rooted in a conscious respect for transcendence, for its
immense and ever-renewing possibilities. The *freshness*
n their lives refreshes us.

It is something we know without asking. The Vietnamese
say, "The will of heaven is revealed in the eyes of the
people." Yes. And in the eyes of some people we see it
more clearly. When we look closely at them, we see not
sainted ones, but ourselves.

How does a prayerful person live? I count five ways.
A prayerful person is attentive to structures of goodness,
alive to the tragic, on top of fear, ready to laugh, and
articulate in the Word of God.

The habit of cynicism comes easily to us. What is difficult
is faith. Faith in anything requires more courage than the
doubt of everything. What matters in an age when so
much has been shown to be corrupt is the habit of seeing
what is good.

I am thinking of the people who, without destroying

us or handing us over to guilt, enable us to move beyond our usual disbelief to a sense of the goodness of what is. Of everything. Of ourselves. Of the world. In an age of massive and institutionalized falsehood, a prayerful person is one who knows and teaches that truth still happens. Human beings have an appetite—indeed, a hunger—for simple acts of honesty.

Prayer is the capacity to touch one's own basic truthfulness and to find it in others. We are so accustomed to duplicity that perhaps the most powerful expression of the transcendent in our midst occurs when the lie is banished from human intercourse. When we are in the presence of the simplest act of truthtelling, we are in the presence of what is beyond us.

Think of the story of the naked king. When the youth finally points out what everyone has been afraid to say—"By God, the king has no clothes on!"—the scales fall from everyone's eyes. The encounter with God is often described as an experience of recovery from blindness (Paul, the beggar at the gate, Gautama Buddha). Seeing things as they are—this is the first effect of prayer. The current crisis in American leadership, for example, is nothing if not the confrontation by the American people of the truth about what their government has become. By God, the king has no clothes on! The act of seeing the truth redeems the common condition of nakedness.

The structures of goodness to which the prayerful person attends include the infallible human instinct for community. In an age of dispersal, loneliness, and massive alienation, the gift of transcendence comes to us when we discover how the communion for which we long does, in fact, survive in us and among us. Prayer opens human beings to the One Life at the root of all separate lives. The prayerful person refuses to settle for the grim predictions of ultimate loneliness that others proclaim and that even find echoes in his or her own soul.

I am not talking about a naive or frightened clinging to clubbiness, or about the stubborn defense of institutions that may in fact be dead. Some cherished communities of ours are dispersed, irreversibly so. I am talking about the rare sense that the passing of the old associations and alliances can be the condition of an explosion into deeper community. The prayerful person helps us prepare to live in a new age, an age in which the human genius for coming together will take postnational forms, post-ecclesial forms, postindividualist forms.

Communion exists. It is a structure of goodness that supports the human effort not to be alone. This sensibility must be rooted in an experience of and a faith in what religious people call the divine communion, the life of God that is the heart of existence. Because the prayerful person breathes the oxygen of that life, he is ready for the ordinary struggle of daily use that makes human togetherness (family, church, *polis,* world) not only possible but mandatory.

The prayerful person is easily recognized in this context. He or she is the one who, having the habit of attention to the structures of goodness, calls the best out of us, not the worst. God's life in the world always has this consequence; we are always ready to make the best of what is given. Not the worst. It proceeds from the conviction—admittedly hard to sustain lately—that what is given is good and full of possibilities for beauty, truth, community, and justice. It is the conviction that at the heart of the world is the act of I AM. Such a sensibility is not automatic. Our own cynicism reveals how easily one can slip into the expectation of disaster. The prayerful ones among us invite the rare and precious response. They invite us to respond to the given goodness with artful goodness of our own.

A sense of goodness, of course, is not enough. We live after Auschwitz, after all. And after Vietnam. And before God knows what. A prayerful person lives deeply in touch with his own and the world's own troubles. He feels the pain of human life intensely. That is not the same thing as the cynical embrace of melancholy. It is not chronic depression. In fact, cynicism and depression are part of our contemporary tendency *not* to feel the pain of human existence. The problem is not that we hurt so much, but that we are so drugged we don't really hurt at all.

Drugged by superficial entertainment, by false religion, by government manipulation. Drugged by drugs. Sensibility of every kind is dulled. We leave without saying goodbye. We grow up without touching each other. We prefer the silence of steel to the small arguments that teach us how to live with and love what is different. We carefully avoid certain neighborhoods and certain topics of conversation. We hope to die suddenly, so that we won't have to deal with that final goodbye either. Prayer works against us in this. Prayer is no drug. Prayer does not ease the pain. It makes us face it squarely. And forces on us the discovery that human pain, to put it most simply, hurts.

"Attention must be paid!" Willie Loman's wife cries on behalf of her desperate husband in Arthur Miller's

Death of a Salesman. The prayerful person says it for all of us. Attention to the dashed hopes. Attention to the effect in us of demonic forces of racial and class and national warfare. Attention to the constitutional inability of good people to do good things. Attention to the widespread habit of broken promises. Attention to our weary, uneasy consciences. Attention to hunger. Attention to the I AM NOT and to the one fully trustworthy event, death.

The sense of the tragic is far from a surrender to despair. Quite the reverse is true. Only a person who profoundly hopes can dare to pay the kind of attention tragedy requires. Praying is the act of embracing human suffering, not in order to wallow in it, but to, in John's phrase, "lift it up." To hand it over.

The prayerful person has discovered that in facing evil and sin, one's own and the world's, there is an opening on transcendence, toward what is totally Other. That opening is the source of hope. In the facing of sin itself is the transcendent promise of forgiveness. In the facing of evil is the possibility of an ultimate goodness that banishes the impulse to surrender. The prayerful person has moved beyond pessimism to real pain and beyond optimism to real hope. He or she disturbs us and consoles us at the same time. The prayerful person is the one in whose presence we can no longer deny our own deep hurt and fear. And in whose presence we no longer need to.

As we saw earlier, suicide is the consequence of the habit of saying no to invitations—simple ones. Do you want to go to a show tonight? No, I'd rather look at the wall outside my window. Do you want to come with us to the meeting? No, I'll just wait here in my room. Do you want to come to earth? No, I'm going to heaven.

The times put the most crucial invitation to us. When massive cultural mutation occurs, the question is: Do you want to be part of the new species? We are taught and tempted to reply, "No, I think I'll just become a fossil." Fossils are safe, clean, polite, obedient, and highly respected in some circles. New species are unruly, chaotic, awkward, and always troublesome to themselves and others. The times face each of us with such a choice. Culturally. Religiously.

The prayerful person, while not liking the crunch of such decisions any more than the rest of us, experiences it, at a deeper level, as the most marvelous invitation to adventure. I think of the four-footed creature that stood on the edge of a primeval forest at just such a previous moment of mutation. It had to decide whether to stay in the familiar shadows and safe confines of a known world or to break out into the open, sunlit savanna of its first uncharted horizon. Some of the four-footed creatures chose to stay behind. Others broke for the far edge of sky, learning how to run and, in the process, leaving safety and their toes behind. The bold ones took on hooves and became horses. And teachers. They teach us.

A prayerful person lives in touch with the kind of secret peace that enables him or her to welcome such adventure. A time of massive doubt, change, and collapse like ours is experienced finally as a privileged moment in which something new can happen. Prayer is attention to the fundamental structures of being that make the dare toward a new kind of being possible. Prayer develops in us the sense that our whole act of existence is held in such a delicate, fragile embrace by someone not ourselves as to make every choice adventurous, shot through with risk. Safety is an illusion. There is no avoiding boldness. And there is reason to trust what we do not control. Fear is the product of our illusion that we control the past. We do not. It is the product of the illusion that human life can be timid. It cannot be. Every moment is the moment of mutation. The new species is continually being born. There is only contingency and possibility. Prayer teaches that.

Prayer nurtures the readiness to laugh. We are so dreadfully solemn about our lives, when in fact they are hilarious. We continually wrap our eyes with tissue paper and call it the world. We are so careful to avoid the broken glass on the sidewalk that we step in the dirt left by dogs. And then we take our bad luck as a sign of ultimate futility. But now and then we get the better of ourselves and chuckle. Or the best of ourselves and laugh. We are so marvelously human, thank God, who is so marvelously Other, thank God again.

The prayerful person laughs. If one doesn't—or worse, is offended by laughter because it is irreverent—he or she is not one of those I am talking about. Laughter is one of the best barometers of prayer. I have been talking all along about the prayerful person's knack for living in touch with the fundamental level of things—where truth, peace, forgiveness, contingency, and goodness all grow out of and open to the Other who is so inexorably beyond. At that level the ridiculous washes over us—and not only the ridiculous, but the delightful. The laugh I am talking about is not the grim snicker of the absurdist, nor the cackle of the failed idealist. It is simply the twinkling appreciation of our ironic situation.

The prayerful person enjoys. Enjoys himself or herself. Enjoys the collision between high-flown rhetoric and the dusty demands of daily living. Enjoys the continuing survival of human life despite itself. Enjoys the patient Other, who always welcomes the return of his loved ones from practicality and despair, from big plans and new saviors. Prayer is the sense, finally, that God enjoys us. Likes our company. Finds us interesting. Prayer teaches that we receive more of God's good humor than of his pity.

The prayerful person has the sense that nothing is ultimate but God. Not even the world. Prayer invites the capacity to stand aside from our own struggle, even our struggle for a humane and just society, and to know that it too is subject to the judgment and embrace that is beyond it and is of God. There is an immeasurable freedom that comes of belief and its practice in one's life. It is the freedom that is the true heart of involvement. God lives. God saves. The world passes. We pass. God saves the world. God saves us. Knowing that we can be irreverent, rebellious, foolish. And this knowledge turns us back to the world, not away from it. We judge, embrace, enjoy, condemn, and love the world. And we are full of the humor that is the other side of pain.

Prayer is the articulation of the Word of God. When Daniel Berrigan was asked how it happened that he still spoke so easily in the words of Scipture, he answered, "It's the only language I know." The prayerful person not only lives in touch with the One Life that is at the heart of existence and Other to it, he or she insists on describing that One Life in the words that we get from our mothers and fathers, beginning with Sarah and Abraham.

Prayer is not simply "sensitivity to the deeper things," not just "reflection" or "meditation." Prayer springs from one's own history. It requires a specific language. It issues in a specific tissue of beliefs and habits. For us that is a matter of Jewish-Christian peoplehood. The experiences of truth, tragedy, and humor demand to have their stories told. We tell them to each other and to God when we pray. The prayerful ones know the stories and the words they wear for clothing. In our case, psalms, songs of the ancient people, tales of the prophets, poems of distress and celebration, the gospel of Jesus, ritual, sacraments, and Hail Marys.

The words of the people who are carried by the Word of God have become the only words of the prayerful person. He or she accepts the discipline of keeping them alive, of carrying them in the heart, of being judged by them, and of hurling them in judgment at corrupt power. Any language can be forgotten. Certainly the language of God's Word can be; most of us seem to be constantly in the process of abandoning it. Indeed, we do it whenever we abandon a human word. We do it whenever we deny the name of God with the I AM NOT. But God is the one who invades the word again and again, forcing it up from silence and forcing us up from falsehood.

The prayerful person teaches us, makes us want to return to the old book, the old story, to reclaim our own first discovery of our names in the name of God. For some of us that is always and especially a matter of remembering Jesus of Nazareth as the way, the truth, and the life. What little we know of prayer we learn from *his* prayer, from his life and its adventures, rebellions, and troubles, and its plunge into the uncharted prairie of a new world that even now opens before us. It all comes down to his life, his death, his life to the full. Prayer depends on the sense that Jesus' life does not end with death or even with resurrection, but continues in our deaths and in our resurrections. The question we asked before—Does the life of Jesus now matter at all?—is its own answer. No death, no doubt, no failure of nerve, no success, no final victory can exempt us from the question's burden, or from the answer's mystery.

We have not yet finished the project of our lives, and so we do not know how the continuing life of Jesus matters. Remembering his prayer to be with and in us, we can only echo it and make it ours.

I have been talking about the "prayerful person" as if there were such people in our midst. People who are alive to the structures of goodness in existence and so praise God for them. People who carry in their hearts the high tragedy of human life and so ask God's help. People who are ready for something wholly new and so thank God for freedom. People who understand their own foibles and ability to mess up nearly everything and so chuckle under God's fond gaze. People who can never finally put aside the memory of Jesus of Nazareth, and so expect that he will return at any moment.

There are people like that. In this season's journey I discover that we are in our own midst. It is me. It is you. It is not claiming so much, prayer. We claim only that, despite ourselves, life keeps wrecking us on the vast and alien shore where the familiar stranger waits with a fish cooking over the fire and bread ready to be broken.

PART FOUR
Adieu

‖11‖

The Law of Return

After a season of remembering, discovering, and re-claiming belief, an identity with church, and a hope in the act of life that holds me, I prepare to return. Return to what? To the United States of America. To Boston, Massachusetts. To a house on Park Street where I live with friends. To my own room on the fifth floor. To saying Mass. To jogging. To eating with students at the university. Tomorrow I return to the life I left. It is like a dream. I cannot wait.

In a few days I will go to New Jersey to give an important sermon. I have been invited by the twenty young men who are joining the Paulist Community this year to preach at the ceremony in which they are welcomed into our brotherhood. What will I say to them? Faced with the impossibility of speaking of this desert and this season, will I fall back on old sermon-tricks? How will I tell them the truth? I imagine myself standing in front of the altar, opening my mouth, and saying nothing. I imagine myself imprisoned by silence. I will be trying to say, "Be careful of your faith in God; it can be lost." But I will also be trying to say, "Do not hoard your faith; better to squander it and live foolishly than to protect yourself and die untested." I imagine the young men looking at me, wondering what I mean, not understanding. But I also imagine them hearing me and saying with their eyes, "Yes, it is that way for us too."

I prepare to return. I collect my papers. I pack the Bible. I am changed by what has happened here. If by nothing else I am changed by having touched the earth where Jesus lived. I have been touched by him. I have crossed a threshold. How to speak of that?

But there is no use pretending that I am not still in the grip of the conflict that brought me here. I have not changed that much. Jesus may have touched the conflict, but he did not take it away. I am the same cynic, the same aggrandizer who prizes sophistication over truth. But I return after having been received by acres of land that *are* holy. And by the edge of desert. By vistas of memory that cling to events that make claims not only on history, but on me.

Since I began this process of turning my questions over as if they were precious coins, the moon has turned itself over nearly three times. Every night I get up from this monk's desk and go out into the wind that has its vengeance on the earth when the sun is gone. The moon watches, and I think it keeps the time for us. Up the road is Abu's bar, where I stored my laughter and learned again to share what is deepest in human beings without talking about it. Across the valley there are the ruins of Herod's castle, silhouetted against the sky, a reminder of the chaos power can produce. Olive trees struggle up the hills toward the other monastery, where a monk shot himself to death. Shepherds' fires blink through the night, flashing at me with the innocence and agony of ten thousand years. Bedouin dogs howl at the wind that lashes them, protesting the armies that surround them, waiting for war, as they have protested against a thousand wars before.

Not having brought a sweater to the desert, I have only a thin blanket wrapped around me against the chill. Someone might take me for a prairie cowboy, standing on a high rock, hair flying, the blanket flapping wildly. I look across at a little town that huddles in the crease between my hill and Herod's. It is Bethlehem. Fortunately, from this distance, I cannot see the souvenir stores or the priest-salesmen. It is easy to imagine three wise men in that setting, but they would probably have to be Arabs; today we would search them for bombs. I try to imagine Yeats's beast slouching toward this moment; instead, there is a neon star over the Church of the Nativity. I see it clearly. At least it does not blink on and off. Nearby is the hermit in his cave overlooking the armed borders of the Jordan Valley. It is hard not to think again of the monk with the tip of the rifle barrel touching his tongue. I shudder, pull the blanket tighter, and turn away.

And here is Jerusalem, showing its night face to me from the top of Mount Moriah. Floodlights push the ancient walls against the darkness, as if to search them for weapons. Jerusalem. It is a name. A secret. A memory. A promise. Jerusalem, whom Jesus would have gathered into himself like a mother her child. His own *pietá*. Jesus would have been *Abba* to Jerusalem. Instead, she gathers into herself the suffering of the universe. Seventeen times destroyed, but there she stands, straddling time, a psalm of golden light. I have not lived or died. I have not been born. Jerusalem knows what life and death are, and I am beginning to learn.

I see the city now as if for the first time. I remember the cynical emptiness with which I toured the holy sites early in the summer. But who am I to claim disbelief so easily? Where has there been real desolation in my life? At *Yad Vashem,* the memorial to the six million victims of the holocaust, an inscription reads: "Forgetfulness is the way to exile. Remembrance is the way to redemption."

I have been remembering. I have been on the way to redemption. The first time I looked at this city I could see only as far as my own overdrawn anguish. Now Jerusalem and its countless agonies are present to me. Turning on my hill, I see Bethlehem and the miracles of birth and re-birth. The night is full of the faces of victims and of children. They see me. I see them. I want to ask their forgiveness. I want to thank them.

I have been changed by the world, which comes at me like a starved dog at night. I turn and unfurl my blanket at it. I break my own melancholy in two with my knee and throw its grim emptiness back at the dark. I say I AM to everything that invites a missed life. I *do* exist. And not only in myself. I am Jerusalem and Bethlehem. I am the suicide monk, the singer in Chile, a mother-poet at the end, an Asian farmer, an Irish outlaw, and a music man about to sing for slain children. The wind rushes off the desert through my veins, drying up my blood. I have been changed by the world, which has its death agony in me. Its shriek to heaven is answered in silence.

If I look at Jerusalem now and *believe* its story, it is

because I have been reporting on that silence as from within it. It *is* possible to lose one's faith in God. It is also possible to remember it. In a summer's journey I have learned God's winter name. The search itself has become his presence. I have stepped back from the exile that forgetfulness is. I have remembered Jesus Christ. Though he is as shadowy as ever, I believe in him. I tell his story. He is the Word of God implanted in my life. I speak him to myself. He speaks himself to me. He is my redeemer and I know it.

I am standing here on the hill overlooking birth and death. It is Tisha b'Av, the late summer feast of Israel. It is the day of mourning for the destructions of the Temple, the first in 586 B.C., over which Jeremiah wept, and the second in A.D. 70 over which Jesus wept in advance. The Temple was the house belief had built, grand and perfect. But it did not stand. Everyone of us whose faith cracks in the night carries the destruction of the Temple in his heart.

And so I must go now to the remains of the Temple to pray. It has taken me all this summer to remember what the world must not forget: God's house is made of flesh and blood. I will go to the holy ruin where we learn to believe it again.

I leave my hill and run down to the ancient road. I hail the Arab bus that roars toward me. I climb aboard and stand in the aisle, though there are seats. The people look at me with narrowed eyes. We hurry up to the Jaffa Gate at the outer wall of the Old City. I get off and push through elbows and stares, past the corner that calls itself the Sixth Station, by the shops with their dripping meat. Beggars look but do not follow. I come out of the

Arab alley to the open space before the Western Wall. Spotlights banish darkness from what still stands of the Temple. A throng of Jews pushes forward to the stone memory of God.

According to *midrash*, when Titus sent his soldiers against Jerusalem, six angels came down from heaven and stood at the top of this wall. At the hour of the disaster they began to weep, and their tears pushed the flames away from the stones. Their tears will continue to flow, *midrash* says, until the Redeemer comes.

On Tisha b'Av the Jews join the angels. They come with their own ruins, each one searched by a soldier whose rifle is slung at his or her shoulder. I cover my head and walk slowly toward that last wall, the remnant, all that is left of what we give to God. My moment of prayer has been a long time in coming. I touch the cover on my head, the wool saucer of belief that protects me from the night, and push through the wailing, bobbing people. They are all in black, all curls. They are the years of exile trying never to forget.

They are the defeat at Masada. Of the last nine hundred Jews holding out against Rome, ten were elected to slay the others rather than surrender. And of the ten one was chosen to kill the other nine, and then to fall on his own sword. Rome's victory was empty, but I think of that one last man. When they turned his body over, his frozen eyes must have been full of faces. I think of the faces I am full of: the monk with the gun in his mouth, the friend nearly drowned after falling from the boat, John Berryman at his bridge, Michele Murray with her family, and Jesus crossing his threshold to the peculiar second birth we know as death.

I approach the stones, confessing my sins against the Jews, against myself, against the flesh and blood God's life is. I am ashamed of my wailing, but still I know that I have lived through the destruction of Jerusalem too. On this night, Tisha b'Av, in the middle of the year's deepest mourning, it is said the Redeemer will be born. It is already true for me. The Redeemer lives in my breast and rebuilds the ruined city I have carried like a curse to this place.

Thousands of black-covered heads moan their private sorrows. I will not forget them. When I return tomorrow to the United States of America in the middle of *its* agony, I will carry them with me. When I stand before the twenty young men who are joining the Paulist Community, I will open my mouth believing that God will have put the Word of this memory on my tongue. I *will* tell them to be careful of their belief, for it can be lost. And I will tell them it can be found again. I will tell them what I learned here: when the great Temple falls, God's praise is still to be sung.

The ghostly moan of all these people rises to heaven. It is the cry of the Arabs who lived in the Wall's shadow before the war. It is the cry of the Jews who cling fiercely to life, having learned its price. I almost see the six angels hovering over us, and almost hear the sound of their weeping. It could also be the song we have come here to sing. The entire creation from the beginning until now resounds in one great act of giving birth. Amid such wailing, memory teaches, the Redeemer is born. There *is* joy. And there *is* music.

At last I reach the Wall. Slowly, I bend, touch, and kiss it.

Everyone moved by the Spirit is a son or a daughter of God. The Spirit you received is not the Spirit of slaves, bringing fear into your lives again. It is the Spirit of sons and daughters, and it makes us cry out Abba. The Spirit and our spirit bear united witness that we are children of God and coheirs with Christ, sharing his suffering so as to share his glory. (Rom. 8:14-17)

James Carroll, a Paulist priest, spent the summer of 1973 studying at the Ecumenical Institute for Advanced Theological Study at Tantur, Israel. This book is an autobiographical narrative in the form of a chronicle of his journey to Israel.

Father Carroll was born in Chicago and received his B.A. and M.A. degrees in theology from St. Paul's College in Washington, D.C. As student chaplain at Boston University from 1969 to 1974, he was well known in the antiwar movement. In 1974 he was playwright-in-residence at the Berkshire Theater Festival.

James Carroll is a widely read poet and essayist. His published books include *Tender of Wishes, Elements of Hope, A Terrible Beauty,* and *Forbidden Disappointments.*